CLIFF HARDY, P.I.

It came to me in a flash, and I reacted instinctively by flattening myself against the wall, pressing back to a long boarded-up doorway. *All the flapping posters had been taken down and nothing had been put up in their place.* The posters would have posed a problem for anyone trying to shoot from farther up the lane. I trusted the feeling of danger; I'd had it too many times before in quiet kampongs and apparently empty paddy fields in Malaya. I sucked in a breath and forced myself to look with one eye down the lane.

The bullet tore a furrow through the bricks a meter or so in front of me and whined off to hit the wall opposite. I heard a sound behind me and turned. A car had turned into the lane and was coming slowly toward me.

Jesus, I thought, *a cross fire. Good planning, men. This is it. . . .*

Matrimonial Causes

A CLIFF HARDY NOVEL

Peter Corris

A Dell Book

Published by
Dell Publishing
a division of
Bantam Doubleday Dell Publishing Group, Inc.
1540 Broadway
New York, New York 10036

ISBN: 0-440-21747-4

Printed in the United States of America

Published simultaneously in Canada

August 1994

10 9 8 7 6 5 4 3 2 1

RAD

For
Roger Milliss,
a sharer in the pleasures of friendship
and the joys and pains of golf

1

I SPRINTED HARD ON THE COARSE SAND OF Dudley Beach, ignoring the camber, jumping over the rocks. I'd be sorry the next day when my ankles and knee joints would remind me of my age, but for now I had no choice—Glen Withers was beating me. Sure, I'd given her a head start, but that wasn't the point. I could see the line we'd drawn in the sand looming, and she still had a lead. She was flagging though; I was pulling her in. I threw myself forward, tripped, dived for the line, and got my hand on it at the same time that her bare foot touched it.

"Draw," I gasped. I'd sprayed sand into my mouth and had to spit it out.

Glen collapsed two meters past the line. Her chest was heaving. "That's not fair. You were falling flat on your face."

I wriggled through the sand toward her. "Win at all costs. That's the motto of the Hardys."

It was a bit past 8:00 P.M. on a summer night. The day had been hot and we'd had several swims and several drinks, made love, and had an afternoon nap. Glen's house was a ten-minute walk away on the rise overlooking the ocean. There was a prawn salad in the fridge and several bottles of Jacob's Creek chablis. We were on holiday—me from my private investigator agency in Sydney, she from teaching at the police academy. Our second summer together and still laughing at each other's jokes. Pretty close to paradise.

We splashed about for a while as the last few people left the beach. Glen wasn't the swimmer she had been. A bullet had left one arm a bit stiff. She got the wound at the time when we first met, back when a case had brought me to Newcastle and Senior Sergeant Glen Withers's father, who was a high-ranking policeman, had been killed. We shared more than the usual number of bonds—an acquaintance with violence, a distrust of authority, and, oddly, the suspicion that relationships couldn't last. We also showed each other our wounds, competed fiercely on occasion, and liked old black-and-white movies.

We walked up the hill and went into Glen's house, one of a set of nine managers' cottages on Burwood Road. The houses are big and simple and perfect just the way they are, but some of the other owners are going crazy with trellises and decks. One has even built a swimming pool, which strikes me as an obscenity so close to the ocean. There ought to be a law.

The sandstone house was cool and quiet. We showered and shared the preparation of the meal, which is to say that I cut the bread and opened the wine. It was good food.

Sneakily, I admired Glen while we ate. She is medium tall with no-nonsense features, all excellently proportioned, and a fine head of thick brown hair. Her hair had gotten fairer in the ten days we'd been up here. She tans but

3

is careful about it and critical of my careless-
ness. I had an Irish gypsy grandmother whose
skin was the color and texture of a well-kicked
football. I'm a bit the same and get very dark
in the summer if I get any beach time. The
recession was still with us—beach time wasn't
a problem. Bill-paying was, but a man with a
woman who has a house on the coast shouldn't
ask for much more.

"Why are you looking at me like that?"
Glen asked.

"Like what?"

"As if you're still hungry and thirsty."

I laughed. Through the open French
doors, an acceptable modification of Glen's, I
could hear the neighbors playing in their pool.
There were loud splashes and laughter. Perhaps a pool wasn't such a bad idea. I put the
heretical notion aside—I was getting up early
and walking briskly to Whitebridge for the paper and then to the beach and back every
morning. A very sound constitutional. Wandering out to swim a few laps in the pool wouldn't
keep the flab down.

I made coffee and, after dabbing on the
insect repellent, we sat out in the backyard to
drink it. The waves slapped on the beach and

the night wind whispered in the tall casuarinas.

"Jesus," I said. "This is good."

Glen murmured something I didn't catch. We were sitting side by side in deck chairs. "Sorry," I said. "What was that?"

"I said you make bloody strong coffee. This is going to keep me awake all night."

"Don't drink it then. I'll dilute it if you like."

"No, it's all right. We've only got two more days. We ought to stretch them. Stay up all night."

I was wakeful too. The afternoon nap had been a long one and I'd only had a couple of glasses of wine. She was right. The coffee was strong, and it tasted so good I wanted more of it. Glen massaged her arm. I moved my chair closer and took over the job, rubbing down the muscle toward the elbow the way she liked.

"How is it?"

"Aches a bit. That's nice. Good holiday, eh?"

"Terrific."

"Did you have any good holidays with Cyn?"

I tried to remember. I'd been married to

Cyn for eight years. We *must* have had some holidays, but I couldn't recall any. No recession back then—maybe we'd been too busy detecting and architecting. I shook my head. "None comes to mind."

"With Helen Broadway?"

More recent history—a battlefield, essentially. "If you can call Hastings a holiday, or Agincourt, or Dien Bien Phu. I went to New Caledonia with a woman once. We had a pretty good time."

"And where's she now?"

Ailsa Sleeman. "She died of cancer a few years back."

"Did you love her?"

"Glen, what is this?"

"I feel like talking. No, I feel like listening. How long have you been a private detective, Cliff?"

" 'Bout twenty years."

"Gee, I was still at school when you started."

"Yeah, in year twelve."

Glen laughed. "Not quite. Tell me about your first case. You must remember it."

"Sure, but Christ, I haven't thought of that in a long, long time."

"What was it about?"

"Back then? Divorce—what else? But there was a bit of perjury, fraud, and murder as well."

2

ALISTAIR MENZIES, I WAS TOLD, CLAIMED
some sort of kinship with the former Prime
Minister, and there was a physical resem-
blance to back the claim. He had the same
height and ponderous build, and he wore the
same kind of double-breasted suits. But his
hair wasn't as white and thick as old Bob's, nor
his eyebrows as dark and dramatic, even
though he apparently did all he could to get
them that way. He was fiftyish and smoked
thick cigars. He was a lawyer, and he gave me

my first job because someone told him I was fairly bright and inclined to be honest.

"This will require some tact, Hardy," he said.

Which you prefer to hire rather than exercise yourself, I thought. "I'm sorry," I said. "I'm going to have to call you something other than 'Mr. Menzies.' You understand why, don't you?"

The bushy eyebrows moved, but without much dramatic effect—framing more of a puzzled frown than an imperious stare. "No, but I was warned you were impudent. I suggest you avoid calling me anything. Be sure to avoid 'mate'—I detest false egalitarianism."

As an opening spar, that made us about equal. I was sitting in one of the leather chairs in his Martin Place office. He had the work to hand out and I welcomed it. I'd been in business for a few weeks now, but there hadn't yet been a cent to deposit in the Cliff Hardy business account. I assumed a neutral expression while he took a puff of his cigar. "As I say, tact needed. You are familiar with the provisions of the Commonwealth Matrimonial Causes Act of nineteen fifty-nine?"

"As amended in sixty-five," I said.

"Quite. This is a divorce case. Our client, Mrs. Beatrice Meadowbank, is suing her husband, Charles. She requires evidence of adultery."

"If memory serves," I said, "she requires a fair bit of evidence—multiple occasions, consistent indulgence, frequent occurrence."

"Are you married, Hardy?"

"Yes." *Tenuously*, I could have added. Cyn and I disagreed about almost everything and fought all the time. We were incompatible but, in our many separations, inconsolable. Neither of us knew what to do about it. My main stratagem was to drink too much; Cyn's was to work too hard as a junior member of the very forward-looking Balmain architecture firm.

"Good, you'll be aware of some of the pressures. Mrs. Meadowbank has reached the breaking point. Her husband is carrying on an affair with a younger woman. Not the first such indiscretion on his part, I might add. We want Charles Meadowbank followed and photographed. You will make a sworn affidavit logging his movements and be ready to give evidence in court."

What was called in the trade a "Brownie and bed sheets" job. I knew they were part of the deal, although I'd hoped to kick off with something more savory—like bodyguarding Shirley Bassey or helping Frank Packer get his winnings home safely from Randwick. I took out a notebook and wrote down the details: description of Meadowbank, home and business addresses, make and model of car, club memberships. A phone call interrupted Menzies's flow, and I took the opportunity to fish out the makings and roll a cigarette. His cigar, placed in a heavy cut-glass ashtray, died. Menzies's pale blue eyes, somewhat buried in the flesh that comes from good living, watched my movements with distaste.

He hung up after grunting into the phone a few times in a well-bred way. "That's nasty," he said.

I exhaled a cloud of Drum. "Smoking? I agree. I plan to give it up when I turn thirty-five. I can't understand why you still do it at your age."

Color flooded his pale, indoors complexion. "I am beginning to regret acting on this recommendation."

I stood up. I like to be on my feet when I'm being submissive. It doesn't feel quite as bad. "I can do the job," I said. "Three assignations should be enough, wouldn't you say?"

"Yes."

"I'll talk to your secretary about my check. See you in court."

"I trust not."

I stopped short of the door. "So it's a bluff? She wants to lead him by the balls to your gentle negotiating table?"

The cigar, relit, was waved imperiously. "You have your instructions, *Mister* Hardy."

All even. Two sets each. Fifty up and both on the black. I renewed my acquaintance with the queen of the outer office, a severe-suited dragon named Mrs. Collins. I signed something I didn't read and got a check for $150—a retainer against my fee of $40 a day, expenses to be submitted on conclusion of commission. Wealth! Prospects! I walked out into a sunny Martin Place and took off my tie. I loosened the top shirt button and opened the suit jacket. Lightweight suit, my one and only. I rolled up the tie and stuffed it into my pocket. I don't know why, but I've always associated neckties with nooses. Maybe it comes of watching too many matinee westerns at the Maroubra Odeon.

As I strolled among the lunchtime crowd, self-employed, a semiprofessional like many of them, I reflected on the chain of events that had brought me to this point. After a stint in the army I'd gone into insurance investigation. I met Cyn when I went to sniff around about a fire that had almost destroyed her Glebe studio. I reported that the fire was entirely accidental and that the claim should be paid in full. I'd have said the same if I'd found kerosene tins and wood shavings in every room. Cynthia Lee bowled me over, and we went to bed on our second meeting and were married a few months later.

Cut to our first infidelities, within a year and both of us guilty. Apologies, forgiveness, recommitment, and more of the same. She was battling to finish her architecture degree, having made a late start after flirting with the alternative life-style in a northern rain forest. I supported her. She qualified. I expected gratitude. She plunged into her highly paid, prestigious work. I tired of the office hours and routines and made the break into private practice. Cyn's political principles—or a version of them—suddenly resurfaced and I became a bourgeois individualist, propping up the authoritarian state.

I went into the first pub I found that offered a lunch counter. You can't pry into people's sex lives on an empty stomach. You need something to throw up.

Lunch started late and went on a bit long. I like to watch people in pubs, listen to them, and it's thirsty work. What with the need to deposit Menzies's check, buy film for the Pentax, get the Falcon fueled up, and one thing and another, I barely had time for a quick call to Cyn to tell her that I didn't know when I'd be home.

"Where are you? The pub?"

"At the garage buying gas and oil. D'you realize they still give you the air and water for free? It can't last. I may have to drive around a bit tonight."

"I knew it," she said.

"Knew what?" I was genuinely puzzled. I often found Cyn's remarks cryptic. *What did she know?*

"That you went into this ridiculous business so you could spend more time away from me."

I was flabbergasted. She started earlier and worked longer than any union would ever allow. "You're wrong, love," I said. "I'm doing it because it might be fun."

She laughed, and Cyn's laugh was a better sound than the cork coming out of a bottle or the rustle of money or a wave on a beach. "Okay, Cliff. Have fun. See you when you get back. Is what you're doing dangerous?"

"Naw."

"Take care just the same. 'Bye."

And that's the way it was with us. Right hooks and kisses. I wanted to go straight to her office, rush her home, undress her, and declare my undying love. Instead, I drove to my office to pick up the camera and make some notes on the Menzies/Meadowbank assignment, the way the Commercial Agents and Private Enquiry Agents Act of 1963 requires you to do.

The office was in a building in St. Peters Lane, Darlinghurst, a bit back from William Street, a bit down from King's Cross. I'd taken out a six-month lease a week ago. It was two floors up, with a desk, a phone, a chair, a filing cabinet, and one dirty window. Other than that, there's nothing to say about the place except that it was cheap. No, there is more to say. I figured it was good territory—anyone streetwise and tough entering there wouldn't turn a hair. Anyone *pretending* to be those things would turn plenty of hairs. And I wasn't expecting too many blondes in Dior dresses. I anticipated that most of my business would come to me over the telephone. So far, I'd been 100 percent right.

Mrs. Meadowbank was away for the week, and Mr. Meadowbank was expected to stray. I caught up with him in Surry Hills. He ran a finance company called Meadowbank Credit, and he wasn't hard to spot coming out of the parking lot—big gray Mercedes, arrogant tilt of the head as he waited for the traffic, brusque, impatient driving style. I followed him to his flat in Bellevue Hill—Birriga Road, as you'd expect, overlooking Bellevue Park. Medium-size block in a garden setting with terrific views, ample car parking, and tight security. The Mercedes sailed into harbor, and I settled down to roll a supply of cigarettes and perfect the most essential part of the private detective's trade—waiting and not falling asleep.

Meadowbank emerged at seven thirty on the dot. He'd had time to shower, slap on the cologne, change his shirt and socks, and check the wallet. I followed the Mercedes to a block of apartments in Rose Bay. Not up to the Birriga Road standard, but not bad. Old-style, red brick, spacious balconies, and a good view of the boats. Meadowbank jockeyed the big car into a tight space with a fair bit of wheel turning and tire torturing. He looked flustered when he got out and wiped his face with a handkerchief. He was a stocky, fleshy type with horn-rim glasses and iron-gray hair. His suit matched his car for color and cost. The finance business must be doing all right. Mrs. Meadowbank was looking at a nice slice.

I registered this as I drove past, looking for a spot for my more modest vehicle. I found one farther down the street, unpacked the camera, and came back to take up a position behind a plane tree across from the flats, which carried the name "Lapstone." The house Cyn and I bought in Glebe was called "Waterloo." Cyn took the nameplate down, saying that it was corny. I'd quite liked it and, as things were shaping up, it was appropriate.

I took a sighting on Lapstone. Despite daylight saving time, which had just been introduced that month, the light was starting to fade under an overcast sky. The light in the street was poor, but there were bright coachman's lanterns mounted over the doors to the flats. And I had fast film and a fast lens. The developer would have to push a bit to get good definition, but I felt pretty confident I could get a reasonable shot of Charles and his companion as they came through the door and a series of photos as they made their way to the car.

If they came. I suddenly realized that I was making an assumption. It was a mild night, late spring, with an evening breeze. The wife was away. Surely they'd go out to eat, get a slight buzz on before coming back to commit the offense of adultery. Charles looked like a man who didn't stint on his pleasures. But what if I was wrong? What if his squeeze had everything set up for fun and games inside? Candles and champagne and silk sheets. I took another look at the block of apartment buildings. A bastard to breach. I didn't even know which flat he was in. Unless they came out onto a balcony and canoodled in the open air, I was stymied.

I wanted a cigarette the way I always did when faced with a problem. I fought the feeling down and considered my options. Even a contortionist couldn't have got a shot including the license plate of the Mercedes and the front of the flats. And what was that worth anyway? I anticipated Alistair Menzies's contemptuous smirk. I could scout the block, maybe get a line on who lived there. I wasn't looking for Brigadier and Mrs. Top-Drawer, after all. But it felt scrappy, not semiprofessional. There were at least six buildings on the block. I tried to tell myself that I'd achieved something—found an assignation point, a field for further investigation. I wasn't convinced.

Minutes ticked on, but fewer of them, I found later, than I thought. Truth to tell, I was nervous, and that distorts the sense of time. I was anxious not to screw up my first job.

"Patience, Cliff," I muttered. "Turn your weaknesses into strengths."

That's when I became aware of the movement in front of me. It wasn't much, just the half-caught motion of a branch, a lightening or deepening of shade. I'd fought Chinese guerrillas in Malaya and learned to take notice of things like that because my life depended on it. There was someone else watching the flats, someone positioned closer than me. I squinted in the failing light, trying to isolate the spot. Not near the tree opposite mine on the other side of the street, not in the narrow garden in front of the flats, but somewhere. Two tall trees flanked the entrance to the driveway marked RESIDENTS ONLY. Poplars with bushy trunks. Maybe there.

I wasn't really alarmed. When I'd worked as an insurance investigator it wasn't so unusual to find more than one guy operating on different sides of the same street. You suspect a worker's compensation claimant of faking and set out to prove it. He suspects his insurance company's bad faith, and you have competition and confrontation. It happens all the time. I had the range and was pretty sure the movement was in the poplars, when Charles Meadowbank and his companion came out of the building. She was a tall brunette wearing a blue silk dress that shimmered as the overhead lights caught it. High cheekbones, sculptured features, upswept hair. I got the camera into position.

The woman stumbled as she reached the first step. Meadowbank, who was directly behind her, stepped quickly forward and around her to help. Then he crumpled and fell down the steps as two bullets blew his head apart.

3

I WAS MOVING WHILE THE SOUND OF THE shots was still reverberating. I shouted and ran forward as the gunman emerged from his hiding place. Time blurred and images shimmered and sound distorted. I threw the camera like a fielder trying to throw down a runner. The shout froze him; the camera hit his shoulder and jerked him out of his murderous concentration. He was small, wearing dark clothes and a stocking mask—I registered this in an eye blink of time—and, I was soon to discover, incredibly quick. I was rushing across the road, six feet one and 170 pounds of frightened, bellowing, missile-throwing force, and he seemed to have all the time in the world to turn and assess his situation. He took off like a top athlete exploding out of the blocks.

I took a few steps in pursuit, but I'd done enough schoolboy sprinting to know when I was outclassed. He was all jet-propelled survival instinct, and I was puzzled and already running out of fuel. Lights were going on in windows, voices were being raised, and I could hear the twittering, muttering sounds of fear for life and property. I was operating on adrenaline at that point, but it was time to switch to something else. Things had gone seriously wrong on my very first assignment as a private investigator.

People shrank away from me as I went back to the front of Lapstone. I ignored them. The tall brunette was sitting on the steps. There was blood and brain matter all over her dress, and her face was a ghastly white under the harsh lights. Meadowbank lay like a broken toy on the bottom couple of steps. His face was only slightly disfigured—a collapsed eye socket and a wound near his jaw—but the back of his head was a mess.

An elderly woman with more presence of mind than most weighed up the situation. "I've called an ambulance and the police," she said to me. "I saw what happened."

"Good," I said. "The police will need to talk to you."

"I saw you throw something. What were you doing there on the other side of the road?"

I didn't answer. The woman on the steps was sitting rigidly, clutching her handbag, and staring straight in front of her.

"Could someone get her a blanket or a coat or something?" I said. "She's in shock."

There was a murmuring in the growing crowd. A few people broke away and someone came back quickly with a big knitted shawl, which was placed over a pair of beautifully shaped, utterly immobile shoulders. I looked around for my camera and saw it lying in a flower bed not far from the poplars. A man was wandering around in that area and he stooped to pick it up.

"Don't touch it," I said. "The police will want things to stay the way they are."

The man looked up belligerently. He was

middle-aged, solidly built, and self-important. "Just who the hell are you?"

I pulled out my private detective license and waved it. I didn't expect it to carry much authority, but it was the best I could do. The elderly woman was offering words of comfort.

"The ambulance will be here soon, Miss Shaw," she said.

Miss Shaw didn't respond.

I saw a metallic glint in the grass—probably a casing from one of the bullets that had killed Charles Meadowbank. The crowd was milling and rumbling, moving restlessly. The glint vanished as someone trod the object into the lawn. The cicadas suddenly burst into their concentrated racket, and then we heard the sirens. There was a collective sigh of relief. I looked at Miss Shaw. Our eyes met for an instant, but what hers were seeing I couldn't tell.

The client of a private investigator has no right of confidentiality, and the detective himself has no protection from the ordinary processes of the law. The uniformed men who came to the Rose Bay crime scene treated me about as roughly as I expected. The elderly woman, who gave her name as Mrs. James Calvert, tried to tell the cops that I was a sort of hero who'd tried to intercept the gunman. Trouble was, she was old and confused and more concerned about Miss Shaw than anything or anybody else, so she made me sound more like an accomplice. I said as little as I could, waiting for the plainclothes boys to arrive.

The senior constable didn't like that either, and we were close to going toe-to-toe when the police from the Darlinghurst station turned up.

Detective Sergeant Colin Pascoe was a big-gutted man with a boozer's nose and late-night eyes. He was a long time out of uniform himself, and he knew all the right moves. He'd brought a photographer with him, and, after the scene was captured on film from every necessary angle, he allowed the ambulance men to take Mr. Charles Meadowbank—provisionally identified by yours truly, confirmed by an examination of the contents of his fat wallet—away. He introduced himself and took my ID folder. Then Pascoe delegated the uniformed men to get names, addresses, and brief statements from the audience, whose enthusiasm was rapidly waning as Pascoe's quiet efficiency undercut the drama. He sent his younger, slimmer assistant off to get Mrs. Calvert's eyewitness account down pat.

Another car with a blue flashing light pulled up and a uniformed policewoman stepped out. She gave Pascoe a nod and went straight to Miss Shaw, adjusting the knitted shawl, taking the young woman immediately under her wing. They went up the steps and back into the apartments. I was left standing on the path with Pascoe, who was swinging a plastic bag containing my camera.

I pointed to the patch of grass. "There's a shell casing trodden in there," I said.

"We got it," Pascoe said. "Must have dug it out while you were eyeing the babe with the big tits." He flipped open his notebook. "Miss . . . ah, Virginia Shaw of this address."

I reached for my ID folder, which he held, half-extended toward me, in his other hand. "If you say so, Sergeant."

He retracted my property with a smile and a cardsharp's snap. "In the car, Hardy. Now!"

* * *

Although a private investigator has no clout himself, it helps if his client is a lawyer. That's when the grease can start to oil the wheels. Pascoe sat me down in an interrogation room in the Darlinghurst station. We sat on opposite sides of a rickety table, and he looked amused when I pulled out a couple of bedraggled cigarettes.

"Planning a bit of sitting and waiting, eh?"

I lit one of the smokes. "More like standing."

"Even worse. Want to tell me what you were doing there?"

I'd taken the precaution of picking up one of Alistair Menzies's cards in his office. For an answer I simply put the card on the desk.

"I might have known. And I expect you're good mates with an assistant commissioner or two?"

I puffed smoke and considered. "I know a detective named Grant Evans."

"He's Armed Holdup. This is Homicide.

Unless you happened to hear the shooter ask Meadowbank to stand and deliver?"

"I'd rather not say anything more until I clear it with Mr. Menzies."

Pascoe went away and left me in the empty, cream-painted room with my cigarettes, a lighter Cyn had given me, and my thoughts. Pascoe had left my license folder on the desk, and I put it back in my pocket. After that, there wasn't much to do except smoke and think those thoughts. I quickly tired of that. I looked at my watch and was surprised to see that it was less than two hours since Charles Meadowbank had set off for Rose Bay. Long trip. Another hour went by before Pascoe returned with a man whose face I recognized but couldn't place.

"I'm Vern Morris, Mr. Hardy," he said. "From Mr. Menzies's chambers."

I nodded. One of the outer-office minions.

"Mr. Menzies has authorized you to make a full statement to the police."

"Big of him," Pascoe said. "Thanks, Mr. Morris."

Morris departed, and Pascoe plunked a battery-powered cassette tape recorder down on the desk. He turned it on and propped the little microphone up on its foldout stand in front of me.

"All modern conveniences," I said.

Pascoe squinted at a needle quivering in a small dial. "You're on."

I told it as briefly and accurately as I could. Pascoe interrupted me to ask whether I had a file on the case in my office. I said I did and he raised an eyebrow. He stopped me again after I'd described the shooting.

"Description of the assailant. Take your time."

"Small, five six or seven, with a light build."

"Pity you didn't get to grips with him. Big bloke like you could probably have cleaned him up."

"He ran like the wind."

Pascoe grunted. "And he had a gun, of course. Did you see the gun?"

"No."

"Okay. Description, continued."

I paused. "Dark clothes, jeans I think, and running shoes."

"Features?"

I shook my head. "Stocking mask. You know what that does to a face."

"Yeah. One fish looks much the same as another. So, a very professional hit."

"I guess so."

Pascoe added some identification remarks to the tape and then stopped it. He took a pack of filters from his pocket and lit up. He offered me one, but I refused. I'd smoked too much already, and smoking filter cigarettes is like drinking decaffeinated coffee—what's the point?

"Any thoughts?" Pascoe said.

"About what?"

"Come on, Hardy. When I said it was a professional job you sounded doubtful."

I shrugged. "I've never seen one before."

He butted his cigarette. "Okay, we'll type this up and you can go after you sign it."

That happened. I caught a taxi back to Rose Bay. A television crew was packing up after filming outside Lapstone. A few people were standing around talking, and a lot of lights were burning in the flats on both sides of the street. It had been the most excitement they'd seen there in years. I kept well away from the action. I was feeling tired and flat.

My face was bristly and my mouth was sour after the smoking and talking. I was hungry and I needed a drink. I looked up at the flats and wondered how Mrs. Calvert and Miss Shaw were doing. None of my business. I got in the Falcon and felt around for the flask of Johnny Walker I keep in the glove compartment for cuts and abrasions. After a few pulls I felt better, well enough to go home to the loving arms of my wife.

"You're drunk," Cyn said.

"No. Just a little lubricated on an empty stomach after a very tough night."

The house was a standard end terrace—two rooms and a kitchen on the ground floor, three bedrooms above, lean-to laundry, and bathroom. It needed work, but the architect member of the team never seemed to get around to thinking about it. We went into the living room and I flopped into a saucer chair.

"You look terrible. What happened?"

I told her. Give Cyn her due, she had a vivid imagination. I could see her visualizing the scene.

"Jesus," she said. "You could have been shot."

"He wasn't after me."

She stood behind my chair and massaged my neck. "Have a shave and a shower. I'll make you an omelet."

A shave and shower at that time of night meant I'd be doing more than eating an omelet before Thursday was done.

4

IN THE MORNING, OVER HERB TEA AND muesli for her, coffee, toast, and Drum for me, Cyn told me about the job she had lined up in Cairns.

"Town houses alongside canals," she said. "A real challenge."

"Like building Venice. Are the houses actually in the canals or what?"

"Cliff, don't be a smart ass. It's interesting and it's only six weeks this time."

"Go with my blessing," I said. "Maybe

you can get us one of the town houses as part of your fee. They gave my mum a flat in the block they built when they knocked down our semi in Maroubra."

"Your semi and ten like it. All undistinguished."

"She died two years later."

"Cliff, she was sixty-eight and she'd smoked thirty a day for fifty years."

"True, but I still blame the architects."

Our fights could build out of exchanges like this. Cyn was a lower north shore girl, a doctor's daughter who'd thrown off the trappings but still trusted bank managers and private school principals in her heart. But there was no fight in either of us today. The memory of the night's lovemaking was too strong and the thought of a six-week separation made us both a bit clingy. She was flying north in twenty-four hours. She went to her office to finalize the details and I went to mine, hoping for a little quiet summons serving or money minding. I anticipated a call from Alistair Menzies's office requesting a refund—not an auspicious start on my new career path.

The morning passed slowly, and when the phone rang I was thinking about money.

The Pentax was a robust camera, but I'd thrown it hard and although it had ended up on grass I wasn't sure that it hadn't landed somewhere harder first. There was likely to be some damage. Tricky case to argue as a legitimate expense, but it was worth a try. However, the voice that came on the line wasn't that of Mrs. Collins, the dragon lady.

"Mr. Hardy, this is Virginia Shaw."

No flies on Cliff. "Would that be Miss Shaw of the Lapstone Apartments, Rose Bay?"

"That's right."

"You had a very nasty experience, Miss Shaw. I'm sorry."

"I did, and I would like to speak to you about that."

"I suppose you know why I was there. I don't quite see . . ."

"That doesn't matter. I don't care about that. I saw what you did."

"I didn't do anything."

"You yelled. You threw something and hit him. You frightened him, and you ran toward him. That was very brave of you."

"I was just surprised, Miss Shaw. Just reacting instinctively. I might've jumped behind a tree next."

Her voice was low and controlled, like that of a dynamic actress playing a reined-in part. Ava Gardner, say. "I don't think so."

"Well, I'm glad to hear that you're all right," I said. "I hope the police didn't give you too hard a time."

"Mr. Hardy," she said, "I want to see you. I was told you are a private detective. I want to engage you. I'm very, very afraid."

Conflict of interest didn't cross my mind. Mrs. Meadowbank didn't need a divorce anymore. I drove to Rose Bay and parked pretty close to where I'd been just twelve hours before. Everything looked unnaturally clean in the street. A water wagon and the sweepers had been through not long before and any residue of the night's activity, like cigarette butts and chewing-gum wrappers, had been cleaned away. The steps in front of Lapstone had been hosed down too. The patch of grass had been chewed up by big feet in heavy shoes.

I buzzed for Flat 3 the way she'd told me to and spoke my name into the squawk box.

"Come up one flight and to the back," said that million-dollar voice.

Virginia Shaw must have been standing with her hand on the doorknob, because the door opened the instant I knocked.

"Come in. Come in."

The flat was much bigger than I'd expected—a sizable vestibule leading to a wide hallway that led to a large sitting room. There looked to be at least another three or four rooms. The sitting room had French doors opening out to a balcony that overlooked the water toward Point Piper. The floors were polished, the furniture was plain, and there were paintings on the walls. Virginia Shaw fit right in. She was tall and slender. Her white dress was simple and looked as if it had been made for her. She looked so cool, I felt slightly sweaty. Maybe I looked it, or maybe it was just that she was the kind of woman who knows what a man wants to do.

"It's warm in here," she said. "Would you like to take your coat off? And what can I get you to drink?"

I peeled off my jacket and she took it from me. I asked for beer. She told me she only had Flag ale, which was fine with me. She excused herself, and I flapped my arms to free my shirt. Then I admired the view, because there were no books on display to snoop at, no ashtray to invite the smoker, and, to me, furniture and paintings are just things to avoid bumping into or knocking off the walls. The water was a deep blue, as if no storm drain or ship's bilge had ever been emptied into it. The scene left my own water view—a glimpse of Rozelle Bay if you half-climbed the back fence—for dead.

She came back with a tray on which was a bottle of beer and a pewter tankard. There was also a tall glass of pale liquid with lemon slices floating in it. She put the tray on the coffee table, expertly poured the tankard full, and handed it to me.

"Iced tea for me," she said. "I don't drink, you see."

"Or smoke," I said. "Thank you."

"We can go out on the balcony if you want to smoke, Mr. Hardy. I'm asthmatic. Please sit down."

We sat down a few feet apart. I decided that she was too thin and too pale. The skin was stretched tight over her high cheekbones in the approved fashion-model style, but I suspected that in her case the look owed something to poor health.

"I won't beat around the bush," she said. "I'm what is known as a call girl."

I had difficulty not choking on the icy cold beer. The effect was like Billy Graham saying "Shit" and lighting up a Marlboro. I said nothing, concentrating on getting air down my windpipe. She took a sip of her iced tea.

"A very high-class call girl. A very expensive one."

I nodded and drank some more beer.

"I've surprised you, Mr. Hardy. What did you think I was?"

"I hadn't given it much thought, Miss Shaw. An actress perhaps, or a lady of independent means."

"Good. I've made the right impression. What would you say if I told you that my stepfather took my virginity when I was twelve and was my pimp for the next few years?"

"I'd say that was very interesting and then I'd ask why you wanted to see me."

"Because I'm sure that if you hadn't been there last night I would have been killed as well as Charles."

That got my attention. I thought back to the event, tried to remember it like a piece of freeze-frame photography. Pascoe had spotted a hesitancy in one of my answers, and I knew that something about the sequence of actions had puzzled me. Was this it? Had the gunman intended to kill Virginia Shaw? He'd done a good, neat job. Two head shots at that distance, in that light, with a moving target was no easy trick. Had there been a pause, a split-second adjustment before firing again, interrupted by me? It was impossible to tell.

She sat and watched me think. Her cool assurance was beginning to get on my nerves. "Did you tell that to the police?" I asked.

That got to her. She almost bit her lip, then turned the action into something more poised. "No."

"Why not?"

"First, do you believe me?"

"I don't know." I drank some of the beer; I believed in that.

"I *saw* it coming." She mimed the action; a gold bracelet slid down her lean forearm. "He lifted the gun and was pointing it at me. You stopped him."

"It all happened so quickly. You can't be sure."

"Quickly? It wasn't quick at all. I saw it in slow motion. If I close my eyes I can see it again."

She shut her eyes. She was a lady who liked to move her face around to best advantage, and I have to admit it was a great face. Now I could see the subtle eye makeup, the shaping of her eyebrows, the smooth, unlined skin. She was utterly convincing and completely phony at the same time, and I had to laugh. The eyes opened wide, and the look that was in them came from a totally different personality from the one I'd encountered so far. The ice maiden had become the stone lady.

"What are you laughing about? It's true. That little swine was going to kill me. I know it."

"How do you know it?"

"Because I know why Charles was killed. Or I think I do. . . . Oh, God, I thought you might help me."

"I'll be happy to help you if you'll knock off the stunts and poses and tell me what's going on."

She lifted her hand to smooth back her hair, then dropped it. The smile that came next was the first natural one I'd seen. "You're right. I'm sorry. I'm so used to acting the way I'm supposed to, I hardly know what to do with my hands."

"Why don't you have a real drink and we'll go out onto the balcony where I can smoke. That's unless the asthma's just a story too."

"No, that's true. It's all true. All right, we'll do that. How's your beer?"

"Plenty left." I got up and opened the French doors. Then I took her glass out onto the balcony and emptied it into a potted plant. I came back and collected the bottle. I topped my tankard and filled her glass. We sat down on cane chairs in the shady corner of the balcony. I raised my drink. "Cheers, and start from the beginning."

Miss Shaw told me that she'd been recruited to act as a corespondent in the divorce of Meadowbank versus Meadowbank, with Mrs. Beatrice Meadowbank as the petitioner.

"Recruited by who?" I said. I'd rolled and lit a cigarette by this time. I'd noticed a few butts in the potted plant where I'd tipped the iced tea, so I had everything I needed.

She sipped some beer with every appearance of enjoyment, but with her, who could tell? "By a lawyer named Andrew Perkins, who used to be a . . . client of mine. It happens all the time. Mr. A. wants to marry Miss B., but he doesn't want her cited as the corespondent. Someone like me is found and money changes hands, quite a bit of money in my case. Charles wanted a divorce so he could marry someone else. I don't know who, but it was tricky in some way."

"What way?"

"I'm only guessing, but I think the woman might have been married herself."

"Very tricky indeed."

"Yes, well, we met by arrangement, Charles and I, and we . . . committed adultery. Well, he did. I'm not married, so I don't know whether I did or not. Do you know?"

I shook my head. "Go on."

"Charles fell in love with me. He wasn't a fool, he didn't want to marry me or anything. But he didn't want to marry the other woman either. And he didn't want to go through an expensive divorce."

"How did you feel about him?"

She gave me a sample from her catalog of looks—this one meant *Virginia knows the score.* "He wasn't the worst man I ever met, and he *was* one of the richest."

"Okay. What happened next?"

"Charles got very edgy. I'm pretty good at getting men to open up, but I couldn't get much out of him. Just hints, you know? He'd say things like, 'It's all a bit of a mess' and 'They're not going to like it.' "

"Did he mean his wife and her lawyer?"

She drained her glass. I gestured with the bottle, but she shook her head. What else could I do? I poured the rest of the Flag ale out for myself before it got warm, drank some foam, and waited for her answer.

"No. It was more serious than that. I really don't know how to describe it, but he was frightened. Defiant, but scared. I think he was a brave man. That was one of the things I liked about him. I admire bravery, physical courage."

She was one of those women who keep you on the sexual hop. Everything seemed to come back to basics—you, me, male, female. I dropped my cigarette butt into the potted plant mud and cleared my throat. "Meadow-bank felt physically threatened, you'd say? In danger?"

"Yes."

"But he didn't take any precautions. The two of you just walked out of here."

"He kept a gun in his car. I saw it. He tried to hide it from me, but I knew. He really was a good man in his way, Mr. Hardy."

I rolled another cigarette and looked out over the blue water and white sails, thinking about good men. I'd known a few here and there, and Virginia Shaw's description of Meadowbank more or less fit him into the mold: Good men try to minimize the harm they do. I sheltered the flame against the slight sea breeze and got the cigarette lit. Why a couple of lungsful of tobacco smoke helps the mental processes has never been explained to me, but I'm sure it's true. I was convinced now that Miss Shaw had a problem. There were things in her story to check—the gun in the car for one, also some of the arrangements. And she *was* scared. I noticed that she sat well back from the edge of the balcony, and it wasn't just to stay in the shade.

"You didn't recognize the guy with the gun, did you?"

"No, nothing like that. I've moved in some shady circles and known some very unsavory people, but not murderers."

"Meadowbank ran a finance company. That's almost a recipe for making enemies."

She shook her head vigorously; the loose brown hair flew about her head. She was intense now, uncaring of the impression she made. "No! He was killed because of this divorce business. I'm sure of it."

"What do you want from me, Miss Shaw?"

"You'll help me?"

"I'm for hire. If it's legal, I'll do it."

"Legal?"

I swilled the dregs in my tankard. "Arguably."

"I want you to escort me to the airport. I'm going away for a while. Then I want you to see Andrew Perkins and tell him I don't know anything about what Charles was doing or planning. Nothing! I want to be in the clear."

"Is that all?"

"No. I want my bloody fee."

5

SHE LEFT ME ON THE BALCONY AND CAME
back a minute later with a check. I was collect-
ing checks like an autograph hunter. Virginia
Shaw's was half the amount of the one I'd re-
ceived from Menzies, but I had a feeling it
was going to involve me in a little more work.
She was wearing a jacket that matched her
dress. I gathered it was time to go. She went
into one of the rooms and came back carrying
a suitcase and a handbag.

"You were packed," I said.

"Yes."

"Booked your flight?"

She nodded as she made some unnecessary repairs to her makeup.

"You were confident I'd help."

"Not really. I was going anyway. I just feel better knowing there's someone here looking after my interests."

A nice, professional way to put it. She closed the French doors but left the bottle and glasses on the coffee table, telling me someone would be in to clean up. On the drive to the airport she wrote down Andrew Perkins's number and a phone number where she could be reached in Melbourne.

"How long do you plan to be gone?"

"Until I hear it's safe to come back."

It was all pretty unorthodox. I wondered how Detective Pascoe would feel about Virginia Shaw's absence. Presumably she'd be needed as a witness at the inquest, like myself. It wasn't exactly my problem, but it could become so. Unorthodox, but interesting. Much more interesting than factory fires and phony break-ins and disappearing motor vehicles. The arrangement Virginia Shaw had come to with the lawyer was almost certainly unenforceable, but I was curious to see what the shyster had to say when I put it to him.

Miss Shaw had booked a first-class, non-smoking Qantas seat to Melbourne. She checked her luggage through, and I accompanied her to the departure lounge. She gave me her hand and I shook it gently.

"Thank you, Mr. Hardy. I have every confidence in you."

"What about the inquest? You'll be called."

She smiled. "That'll be weeks and weeks away, won't it? You'll have everything sorted out by then, I hope."

It sounds dumb, but I made noises that suggested she had the right man for the job. All I can say in my own defense is that she had a strange ability to convince you that what she wanted was both reasonable and in your best interest as well. I wasn't a complete innocent though. I left her well before boarding time to give her the opportunity to duck away and do something different if that's what she had in mind. I watched her from a discreet distance. She looked at the departure board and her watch. Then she went to the newsstand and bought a magazine. When the flight was called she was one of the first through the door.

It was midafternoon. I'd arranged to take Cyn out for dinner, so I had a few hours to fill in. I hadn't heard from Alistair Menzies and it seemed like a good idea to find out how much of his check was still mine. I called the office from the airport and was told that Mr. Menzies could spare me ten minutes at four thirty. I agreed. That gave me time for a sandwich and a quick drink in the bar. I was glad I wasn't a professional if it meant having only ten minutes at four thirty.

On the drive back to the city I decided that my client was suffering from an excess of imagination and caution. There seemed to be no reason why a man would be killed for changing his mind about getting divorced. And any judgment about the assassin's intentions by a woman who'd certainly gone into shock immediately after the shooting was bound to be faulty. I'd extract a promise to pay from Perkins if I could, and that would be the end of it.

Menzies was subdued and preoccupied.

He agreed that the cost of repairing my camera was a justified expense and seemed uninterested in recovering any of his retainer. All he wanted to know was whether the police had mentioned a suspect.

"Not to me," I said.

"Presumably the murderer was hired?"

I shrugged. "Who knows? Depends on what sort of a bloke Meadowbank was. He could have had a hundred enemies, gambling debts, criminal associates."

"He was an eminently respectable businessman as I understand it. Also, unhappily, a philanderer."

"How's his wife taking it?"

"Calmly."

The bushy eyebrows moved, but not in a way to convey any meaning to me. Was he worrying about losing his fee for handling the divorce, or did he think she might be charged with arranging the murder? My ten minutes were up, but he didn't seem to be in a hurry to rush me out, so I thought I might as well put in a little work on my next case.

"Was the Meadowbank divorce on the up and up?"

"I don't follow you."

"I mean, was there any arrangement to provide a corespondent conveniently?"

His jowls quivered. "The Queen's Proctor can be very hard on that sort of thing."

Not an answer, but it saved me a hunt through a divorce-law textbook. Now I'd be able to go straight to the index. As I got up to leave I said, "Do you happen to know a lawyer named Andrew Perkins?"

No mistaking the eyebrow language this time—a scowl of disapproval. "Why do you ask?"

"His name came up in connection with something I'm working on."

"If he is a principal, I would advise you not to touch the matter, Mr. Hardy. Our profession is famous for reticence with regard to the shortcomings of its members. But take my word for it, Andrew Perkins is a barrister and a double-dyed scoundrel."

Dinner in the Malaya restaurant on Broadway went well. Cyn could eat prawn sambal hot enough to fry your socks, and this kind of food always put her in a good mood. Made her horny too. I drank enough Quelltaler hock to push away the feeling that the Virginia Shaw case was going to lead me into difficult territory. We ate in the Malaya often. Customarily, I was facing a day of office-bound boredom and clients' domestic tension thereafter. Tonight was very different. I snapped into a young-and-devoted mood, squeezing Cyn's long, firm thigh, joking and keeping my cigarette consumption—something she hated—to a minimum. I ate one of her red-hot prawns and put on my Peter O'Toole voice, the one he uses when he shows the young airmen how he can snuff out a burning match with his fingers.

"The trick is, my deah, not to mind!"

Tears were coming to my eyes as the chilis seared my taste buds.

Cyn laughed. "I'm going to miss you, Cliff. Don't fuck anyone in our bed. Okay?"

Eleven hours later I was back where I'd been the day before—in the departure area at Mascot Airport. Cyn and I were both a bit hung over, a state that induces introspection rather than concern for others. Anyone watching us might have thought we were friends or business associates, until the boarding call came. We put our arms around each other and hugged hard.

"I'll call you tonight," she said.

"Have fun. Get all the water levels right. Don't forget the tides."

" 'Bye, Cliff."

I watched her tall, narrow figure vanish through the door. Then I dashed to the window and saw her walking across the tarmac to the plane. She wore a blue linen suit, white blouse, and medium heels. Every man in the boarding party looked at her. I waved, even though there was no chance of her seeing me through the smoked glass. She ducked her head as she entered the plane. Six weeks. I wondered why she hadn't suggested that I come up and visit her. The money? *Don't fuck in our bed.* What about other beds? I was as suspicious as hell, and I made it worse for myself by waiting until the plane took off.

I lit a cigarette and watched the clouds swallow the plane. I had a bad feeling about this. I wanted to rush back to the house and check a few things—had she taken her black satin nightdress and the silk pajamas with the leopard-skin pattern that she called her "rooting rags"? And what if she *hadn't* taken them? What would that mean? I shook my head, knowing that these thoughts were profitless. Hangover thoughts, brought on by spicy Asian food, too much wine, and too little sleep. Only one cure. I'd brought a flask of brandy from the house, and I headed for the coffee shop to mix up some medicine.

6

THE AIRPORT WAS BEGINNING TO FEEL LIKE a better place to operate from than my office. It had coffee, a toilet, sinks, telephones, parking space, and it cost nothing to hang around there. I phoned the number Virginia Shaw had given me and got a cool female voice on the line.

"Andrew Perkins and Associates. Juliet Farquhar speaking."

"Miss Farquhar, my name is Cliff Hardy.

I'm a private investigator. I'd like to see Mr. Andrew Perkins as soon as possible please."

"In what connection, Mr. Hardy?"

"In reference to Miss Virginia Shaw."

There was a pause. I imagined her buzzing through to put the question to the boss. It didn't sound like the kind of operation where people actually got up and walked across the room to do things. It occurred to me that I should know where Perkins and Associates was. I started to hunt in the telephone directory.

"Mr. Hardy, are you there?"

I'd dropped the book and was scrambling for it when she spoke. A page tore in my hands and I swore.

"*What* did you say?"

"I beg your pardon. I've . . . spilled my coffee. Yes, Miss Farquhar?"

The coolness was positively chilly now. "Mr. Perkins has no client by that name. Perhaps you have the wrong information. There are a number of legal practitioners named Perkins."

"I'd like to see him anyway."

"Mr. Perkins will be out of Sydney on

business for the next few days. Perhaps you could call back next week?"

"Perhaps."

"Thank you."

She hung up. I continued my search without doing further damage to the phone book. The office of Andrew Perkins and Associates was on Phillip Street. Where else? I knew the old buildings where the legal eagles had their chambers—rabbit warrens of twisting corridors, steel-cage elevators, and solid oak doors. A man could barricade himself inside a place like that, or slip out very easily if he knew his burrow well. It was beginning to look as if I'd have to make a call on Mr. Perkins at home. That would take some work. I wondered if Miss Shaw had anticipated his lack of cooperation. I wondered whether he had come to her, or vice versa, when he was her "client." I wondered a lot of things.

Pleasant as it was, especially with the prospect of the bar opening soon, I couldn't hang around the airport any longer. I drove back to the city with only the intrigue of the Shaw matter and the comfort of a couple of hundred bucks in the bank to keep me from feeling jealous and deserted.

I hadn't gone into the private investigation game without some preparation in the form of a long talk with Ernest Glass, who'd been a private eye since he got back from World War II. Ernie had been an MP for most of his stint, although he'd seen some action here and there. Along with a few tips about getting through locked doors and extracting information from neighbors, he'd had one critical piece of advice.

"Cultivate a relationship with a policeman, boy," he'd said. "Better still, with a couple of policemen, and the less they know about each other the better, if you get what I mean."

I already had a friendship with Grant Evans, who I'd served with in Malaya. It had proved useful while I was working in insurance, but I hadn't tried to widen my net. Maybe this was the time. I drove to the Darlinghurst station and asked to see Detective Colin Pascoe. The desk officer recognized my name from the paperwork attached to the Meadowbank killing.

"You armed?" he asked.

"No."

"We had a fuckin' nut in here yesterday.

Yugoslav, as you'd expect. Pulled out this fuckin' huge gun and threatened to kill everyone unless his missus was brought back to him."

"I don't see any broken glass. What happened?"

The desk man thumped his meaty fist down on the papers in front of him. "They've cleaned up the blood. One of our blokes flattened him, but good. The prick. You'll find Detective Pascoe one floor up and along to the right. Room six."

Down led to the interrogation rooms, up to better things. I knocked on a glass-paneled door and opened it when I heard someone say "It isn't locked."

The speaker was Pascoe—shirt-sleeved, bulging with a combination of fat and muscle, perched on a desk, and abusing someone on the telephone. His assistant of the night before was head down and ass up at a desk, working his way through a stack of files. Pascoe waved me to a chair and with his free hand mimed the action of rolling a cigarette. I took out my tobacco, made two, and handed him one. He dipped his head toward the light. He sucked hard on his first drag and the cigarette was nearly half-consumed. I sat and waited for him to finish his call. The young plainclothesman was expressionless, but taking everything in.

Pascoe banged the phone down. "So, the private dick. The tough guy who rolls his own and chucks things at hit men. What can I do for you?"

I shrugged. "I dunno. Just staying in touch. Thought you might have mug shots for me to look at, might want to talk about an identification parade."

"Bullshit," Pascoe said.

"Menzies wants to know if his client's a suspect."

"That's more like it. Yeah, why not? Tell him there's a lot of self-made widows around. We catch a few of them. Not many. Our investigation is proceeding. Anything else?"

"I was wondering about my camera. When can I get it back?"

"Got some more snooping to do, Hardy? Why don't you earn an honest living? You look like a capable bloke. Evans speaks well of you."

"I'm hoping for better things. The camera?"

Pascoe turned to the younger man. "Why don't you go out and get a cuppa tea, Ian?"

Ian moved with alacrity. "D'you want something, Colin?"

"No, son. Just to be alone with my friend here."

The door closed. "I should've asked him to get cigarettes," Pascoe said.

I started rolling.

"The way things work," Pascoe said, "is that I pass this over to Homicide. But I still have an interest. If I come up with anything and hand it on and if it's useful in some way . . ."

I gave him a cigarette and lit it.

"Thanks. And if it's useful, I can still score points. You follow me?"

I nodded and lit my own smoke.

"You're in my bailiwick, Hardy. St. Peters Lane, Darlinghurst. I can be useful to you or I can be a fuckin' awful nuisance."

"Sure," I said.

"So, have you got anything to tell me?"

The plain fact was, I didn't like his style and I trusted him even less. Ernie Glass would have called me a fool or something worse, but

I stood up and squashed out my cigarette. "No. Nothing. How about my camera?"

"Piss off."

I went out quickly and took the stairs going down three at a time. I waved to the man at the desk and left the station. As I stepped onto the sidewalk I collided with someone coming the other way. We both lost our balance and apologized. It was Pascoe's assistant. I said I was sorry again and moved away.

"Mr. Hardy."

I turned back. He was extending his hand. I shook it.

"Ian Gallagher. I just wanted to say I thought you handled yourself pretty well the other night."

"I don't think your boss agrees with you."

"Colin hasn't got . . . ah, a lot of imagination. Now me, for example, I don't think you came in just to ask about your camera."

"No?"

"I think you might have been looking for a little reciprocity, some give and take. That's not Colin's style. You might do a bit better with me."

He was a medium-sized, fair man with

the Robert Redford kind of good looks. When I examined him a bit more closely I saw that, like Redford, he wasn't quite as young as he seemed. There were slight crow's-feet around his eyes, and his skin was roughened by quite a few summers and winters. His blue eyes had a reproachful look. *Could be a bit of frustrated ambition here*, I thought.

"I haven't got much to give," I said.

"I'll take an IOU. Colin Pascoe'll never get anywhere with this. I've got a feeling about it. There's something subtle behind it. Now, you haven't just dropped it, have you?"

"Not exactly."

"Okay. My guess is you're still working for one of the lawyers or maybe for the widow. I'll give you something. Virginia Shaw, remember her?"

"Miss Shaw," I said. "Meadowbank's companion."

"Right. She gave us a cock-and-bull story about meeting Meadowbank at a business lunch and becoming attracted to him. Hard to picture, isn't it?"

I shrugged. "Ava Gardner married Mickey Rooney."

"Virginia Shaw's a high-class whore. She's

almost a professional co-re. Been up twice already. Three's about the limit in that game before questions get asked. She wouldn't come cheap and she's got some nasty friends."

"Like who?"

He grinned. "That's enough from me. I can see you're interested, which means I was right—you're still involved. So I've got something out of our talk after all. Just remember who to talk to first if you need any help. But the help won't be free. Fair enough?"

He was away up the steps, not waiting for a response. A neat operator. Maybe Ernie Glass would have approved, but I think the idea was to manipulate the cops, not the other way around. Still, Gallagher had confirmed part of Virginia Shaw's story. I walked to Riley Street, where I'd parked. The hangover was a distant painful memory, and I resolved not to do any daytime drinking. In my experience, hangovers are like old boxers, always ready to make a comeback. It was a warm morning, good for walking in the country or a park. Darlinghurst was something different. The money that had come into Paddington and Balmain to tidy up the houses and gardens, pave the sidewalks, and install speed bumps hadn't arrived here. The rows of terraces were faded and forbidding, patched with sheets of iron and plywood, and the plants that grew in the backyards looked as if they'd rather be somewhere else.

Still, I walked a few blocks for the exercise, passing the houses that wouldn't open until the late afternoon, when a woman would sit in the hallway with a magazine and a cigarette, showing her legs and tits, and the ones where pensioners anxiously parted the curtains watching for their checks to arrive. There were shops that sold pies and Cokes to factory workers during the day and marijuana at night, and newsstands where the real selling items were kept under the counter. I felt almost respectable, with an office, a mortgage, and a nearly paid-off car, but there were plenty of men around here lowering the level in their sherry bottles who had once been much more respectable than me.

I unparked the Falcon that was nearly mine and drove the short distance to St. Peters Lane. Parking was a problem around here, and I was in negotiation with a tattooist named Primo Tomasetti to rent a cement slab at the back of his parlor for a modest fee. Modesty was the main subject of the negotiation. I got lucky in Upper Forbes Street and found a decent-size space—probably an ABC worker going to lunch. The thought sent me into a milk bar for a sandwich and a totally virtuous can of soft drink.

I climbed the steps from William Street and turned into St. Peters Lane from Upper Forbes. None of that trendy money had reached here either. The back walls of the buildings that front onto William Street were gray and bare apart from the graffiti and the stuff the bill posters put up—advertisements for rock concerts, boxing and wrestling matches, speedway events, martial arts—all the diversions of the seventies. The posters got ripped and flapped in the breeze like sails. I'd noticed a Van Morrison poster, stuck over a dozen others, that had come adrift and opened out into the lane like a door. I liked Van Morrison and was sorry I'd missed the concert. As I walked up the lane, something felt strange. I tried to register it: No cars where they shouldn't be, no one hanging around pretending to be what they weren't. . . .

I stopped twenty meters away from the door to my building. The lane was usually quiet. A church at the top end on the right, then the ABC premises. Nothing much on the other side. An auto electrician's workshop that had made the place busy in the past had closed down a couple of days before I signed my lease. In my building were an iridologist, an astronomical-chart drawer, a dental technician, and me. Most of the offices were vacant, and it was the same in the other buildings. The area had to be scheduled for renovation or demolition and redevelopment. So, not a lot of traffic, but there was something unnatural about this stillness.

It came to me in a flash, and I reacted instinctively by flattening myself against the wall, pressing back into a long boarded-up doorway. *All the flapping posters had been taken down and nothing had been put up in their place.* The posters would have posed a problem for anyone trying to shoot from farther up the lane. I trusted the feeling of danger; I'd had it too many times before in quiet kampongs and apparently empty paddy fields, but I felt ridiculous—this wasn't Malaya, or Vietnam, or New York City. I sucked in a breath and realized that I'd been holding myself in a sort of suspended animation. Survival stuff. Why not?

I moved my head out of its rigid, locked position and forced myself to look with one eye down the lane. I desperately wished for a weapon, but my Smith & Wesson .38 was locked away in the office filing cabinet.

To use even one eye you have to expose some forehead. I squinted up the lane, prepared to run forward to my doorway. What the hell if I looked ridiculous? I was imagining things. No one was watching. The bullet tore a furrow through the bricks a meter or so in front of me and whined off to hit the wall opposite. I was blinded by the brick dust but still registered impressions. The shot was muted—a silencer. Bad for accuracy, but what use was that to me now?

I heard a sound behind me and used my undamaged eye to look back. A car had turned into the lane and was coming slowly toward me. *Jesus*, I thought, *a cross fire. Good planning, men. This is it.*

The car continued slowly up the lane. It was a sleek green Rover, a respectable person's car. The driver was a fat man, pale-faced, apprehensive.

"Hardy!" The harsh voice came from up near the church. "Leave it alone!"

The Rover stopped. I could feel my fingers crushing the sandwich that was still in my hand into a soggy mess. The driver rolled down his window.

"I'm looking for an auto electrician," he said.

7

IT WASN'T THE FIRST TIME I'D BEEN SHOT at and it didn't leave me weak and shaking, although it was a while before I could peel myself from the wall and go into my building. When I got to my door and fished for my key, I realized I was still holding the food and drink. I put them on the desk and opened the drawer, where I'd installed a cask of red wine. It was a good fit. I filled a coffee mug and rolled a cigarette. A bullet within a meter of the skull cancels out some good resolutions.

The bitter-lemon soft drink just wasn't going to cut it. I smoked the cigarette, ate the squashed sandwich, and drank the wine. All very natural functions and reassuring to be able to perform them. I wanted it to stay that way.

Given that, I had the option of doing what I was told—dropping it. I could return Virginia Shaw's money, tear up her Melbourne number, and get on with process serving and doing character checks for employers and looking for a little light car-repossession work. I could even spend some money, fly up to Cairns, and see if Cyn was cheating on me with someone in a safari suit. A great start to my new, independent life as a small business-man that would be. Two jobs, two messes, and a quick run for cover.

No way. My phone call to Andrew Perkins had produced immediate results. I'd rubbed a few people the wrong way as an insurance investigator and there were those around who didn't like me for one reason or another, but not enough to send a shooter. It had to be Perkins. The intention may not have been to kill me. It was hard to tell, also impossible to prove. Perkins didn't have to go into hiding on my account, but he'd be on the defensive. What was clear was that Detective Ian Gallagher had been right: There was something *behind* the Meadowbank shooting, perhaps something big. I could go to Gallagher and show him . . . what? The chunk out of the wall? The brick dust in my hair?

After another cigarette and a half mug of wine, I'd convinced myself that the personal had merged with the professional and that I should have a meeting with Andrew Perkins. I dug out my slightly out-of-date copy of *Hammersmith's Australian Law List*, one of the tools of the trade, and looked up Perkins. No chance of a private address, but some of the more status-conscious types liked to list their clubs. Perkins's entry named three: the GPS Club—meaning he'd attended one of the major private schools—the Naval & Military, and the White City Lawn Tennis Club. No affiliations with my only club—the Balmain-Rozelle RSL. I couldn't see myself strolling into the GPS Club wearing my Maroubra high school tie, and a brief second lieutenancy gained in the field wouldn't cut much ice at the Naval & Military. But White City was a different matter. Tennis shirts and shorts tend to cancel out class differences, and my father-in-law, Dr. George Lee, was a member.

I phoned White City and was told that the members engaged in social tennis on Saturday afternoons and club competitions on Sunday, weather permitting. It was Friday, and the forecast for Saturday was fine and warm. I phoned Cyn's father at his practice in St. Leonards.

"Doc? Cliff. Lost many lately?"

"No more than usual. Had an extraordinary hemorrhoid just now—big as a cricket ball."

"Wish I'd been there. How's Inge?"

Inge is Cyn's mother—a Danish-born snow queen whose genes dominated Doc's to produce my blond wife. Doc is squat and dark —a case of opposites attracting. Lee is a gypsy name, in some cases, and Doc and I had formed a good bantering friendship over the years based on our common supposed gypsy heritage, sporting interests, and love for Cyn, who is an only child.

"She's fine. Cynthia's gone to Queensland, so I know the two of you aren't coming into bourgeois territory to cadge a decent meal. No trouble I hope, Cliff?"

"No trouble, Doc. I need a favor. You're a member at White City?"

"Mmm, yes. Haven't been down there for a while."

"Ever met a bloke named Perkins? A lawyer?"

"Don't think so. As I say, I haven't played there much lately—too old, too busy."

"You're still financial, I hope."

"Of course. Still the best grass courts in Sydney, and grass is the only surface for the game."

"I agree. Could you find out whether this Andrew Perkins plays regularly and get me in to meet him?"

"How soon?"

"Tomorrow would be fine."

"You're a bull-at-a-gate sort of chap, Cliff. I'll see what I can do. Where are you?"

I told him the office number would get me for the next few hours and I'd be at home after that. I resisted the call of the wine and drank the bitter lemon as I made some judicious entries in a file headed SHAW, VIRGINIA. I made out a deposit slip to bank her check and wrote a check of my own for my NRMA membership, which was due. Paperwork over for the day, a big change from my previous job. I was missing Cyn, or rather the thought of her, already. I didn't have a contact number in Cairns. I supposed I could get one from the office, but why hadn't she given me one? Why hadn't I asked? I glanced around the drab office thinking that Cyn would have been able to brighten it in some way. I hadn't invited her to see it. We weren't in good shape. Doc and Inge would be worried if they knew.

I flicked through a few circulars that comprised most of the mail—install a security system, buy a safe, fit a car alarm. Fear was the name of the game and I was a part of it. I went out of the office and down the corridor to the one bathroom-cum-toilet that services the whole building. I washed my face and combed my hair. I wanted a cup of coffee. There was a broom-cupboard-size alcove near the bathroom with a shelf and an electrical outlet that might work. A hot-water maker, instant coffee, and some long shelf-life milk would raise my quality of life. The phone was ringing in my office and, as I sprinted down the cracked linoleum to catch it, I thought about sprinters and shooters. *Was the guy who shot at me in the lane the killer of Charles Meadowbank?*

Doc Lee had been on the phone to White City and come up trumps. Andrew Perkins was a regular player, a never-miss-it type who could be relied on to be at the courts tomorrow if the weather held.

"A few sets'd do me good, Cliff," Doc said. "I'm putting on weight. Might get me playing more often. Inge will bless you. Mind you, it's her bloody cooking that's making me fat."

We arranged to meet at one thirty.

Leaving me with twenty hours to fill in. I found myself reluctant to leave the office. I didn't like the thought that a gunman could be out there waiting for me. I had a feeling that I was getting involved in something big and complex, and I had no organization—like the army or the Greater Eastern Insurance Company—to back me up. No spit 'n polish, no saluting, no keeping office hours, but this was the price to be paid for independence. My Smith & Wesson .38 Police Special was an eight-shot double-action revolver with a three-inch barrel. It was comfortable to carry and fire and accurate over a short distance. I cleaned and loaded it and put it into a holster that nestles into the small of the back. Pull your shirt-tail out and no one knows you have death sitting just above your left buttock.

Just to be sure, I went up onto the roof to scout the terrain before leaving the building. You can travel a fair distance over the top and get a look down into the side streets and back lanes for a few blocks around. Everything looked normal and quiet. I peered out over the building next door and found myself looking at Primo Tomasetti's empty cement slab. There was a door right next to it and I could get into that building from mine. The idea of renting the space suddenly had a much greater appeal. I locked up and left, and nothing happened. I deposited Virginia Shaw's check just before closing time. No one had booby-trapped my car; no one was lying in wait for me in Glebe.

The empty house depressed me. It had soft spots in the floors, patches of rising dampness, and Cyn and I were forced to move our bed to another part of the bedroom because the ceiling had developed a dangerous-looking sag. A couple of uprights were missing from the stair rail. Cyn had said a dozen times that she'd get them replaced. There are woodworkers who can reproduce the exact shape. I had a feeling it would never happen. Outside was no better. There was enough work in the small front, side, and back spaces to keep an active man busy for days. I sat in the concrete backyard and smoked.

I went inside and called the Melbourne number.

"Yes?" A male voice. Educated, uninterested.

"Virginia Shaw, please."

"Who's calling?"

"Hardy, from Sydney."

A pause of maybe fifteen seconds and then he was back. "Try again in twenty-four hours." The phone went dead.

Intriguing.

I stood under a hot shower, had my second shave for the day, and put on fresh clothes. I strapped the gun on and went to the RSL for a meal and a few drinks. No one followed me coming or going and I won fifteen dollars on the poker machines.

8

WHITE CITY RESISTED CHANGE. THE
grandstands were still made of wood, and a lot
of the courts were like the hallowed center
playing space—grass. It had an old-world air
without any pretension. I saw Sedgman win
the NSW Open there in 1952; Hoad,
Rosewall, and Laver a bit later. Newcombe
and Roach looked to me to be as good as any
of them. I played there myself once, in a
schoolboy tournament. Tom Wild and I were
eliminated in the second round of the doubles.

I wasn't good enough to play singles, but it was still a kick to play with a net that went all the way down to the ground and have the balls collected by someone else. And Doc was right: There's something about the living, breathing surface of grass that makes the game on it a better experience.

I parked outside the complex and wandered in, wearing my whites and carrying a towel and my far-from-new Wilson racket. Doc was waiting for me by the clubhouse. We shook hands and said how good it was to see each other. I meant it. I liked the old boy, with his rough head, stocky body, and no-nonsense manner. He came from a long line of well-heeled professionals, but it didn't seem to have polished him too much. He was as much at home with boxers and jockeys as with Macquarie Street surgeons and Vaucluse socialites. He *had* put on weight though. His stomach stretched the waistband of his shorts and he was fleshy around the neck.

"I'll sign you in, and I think we can get a court to ourselves for half an hour. I'll need that to get the kinks out."

"Me too."

"Then it'll be a couple of sets of doubles. D'you want to play men's or mixed?"

"Mixed."

"Very wise. What about this lawyer chap? Want to play with or against him? I'm told he's a big man, redheaded. Shouldn't be hard to spot, although it'll get pretty busy around here soon."

"Shit, no, Doc. I want to follow him home when he leaves. I wouldn't mind a chance to get a look at him—see whether he can hit a volley or not."

"Hmm. This is all to do with the cloak-and-dagger business you've got yourself into?"

We were moving into the clubhouse—parquet floor, big windows, and several tons of cut crystal, dull pewter, and polished glass. In a prominent place was a picture of John Bromwich executing a two-handed backhand. Totally proper in his long trousers and wrist-buttoned shirt, and utterly unorthodox in his stroke. It was a great photo. Doc introduced me to the secretary of the club, a blazer-clad mustache wearer whose name I instantly forgot. He signed me in as a visitor, and we went out onto the crisp grass of Court 12. Doc had a tin of pressure-tested balls, and we warmed up for a couple of minutes. He had powerful, accurate ground strokes, an erratic volley, and a weak second serve. I was solid on the forehand and weak on the other wing, both at the back of the court and at the net. My serve was a reliable, medium-paced kicker.

We played best of three for service, and I won. I hadn't played for almost a year, since a holiday Cyn and I had had on the south coast, and I was rusty. I served two double faults, fluffed a backhand, whacked a great forehand volley into the corner, but lost the game when I tried to do it again and missed. Doc's second serve was very fat—slow with minimum spin. He had me love–thirty with a couple of good first serves, and then he faulted with the first ball twice and I passed him easily when he unwisely came in. The game went to deuce, and I won it with a good crosscourt forehand and a lucky lob.

We both won our serves and were tied four to four when Doc said we had to surrender the court. I wasn't sorry. Most of the games had gone to deuce with several advantage points—twenty minutes of scampering about in the sun takes its toll when you're out of practice. Doc went straight into a mixed doubles, and after a couple of minutes I was drawn into a men's match with two players about my own level and one—not my partner —a great deal better. More hard work before we lost seven to five. I sat out for a while and ran my eye over the mob, which had grown markedly as lunchtime receded. They were a well-heeled group to judge from the clothes and accessories, the women sleek and most of the men trying to stay that way, with some notable failures. I played a mixed set with a hard-hitting, pretty blond woman who defended me on the backhand side, and we won easily.

I was getting a soft drink from the machine when I spotted Perkins. The club members had their names on magnetized strips that were fixed to a board. As you joined a foursome your strip was taken from the pool and placed on the board. You went back into the pool after the set until your turn to play came around again. A tall man in immaculate tennis clothes and with short, crinkly red hair placed his strip beside three others. He carried two rackets and wore a sweatband—all just a bit showy to my mind, unless he was very good. I removed my visitor's strip from the pool and went with my drink to Court 8 to watch Andrew Perkins, Barrister-at-Law, at play.

He was good, very good. He was a bit bigger than me, about six feet two and around 180 pounds, and unlike me he'd been well-coached and every movement he made was economical and efficient. He warmed up like a professional, going systematically through the strokes and letting his service action warm up slowly. He could hit flat and with topspin off both sides; he had a vicious, swinging serve and he was a tiger at the net. He took longer over the warm-up than the others wanted, and I saw the frowns and body language and fidgeting that gave me an idea of Perkins's popularity. He didn't care. He sharked at the net and his side won the right to serve. He served first and sent down an ace. He won the game forty–love and took the only point that was really contested with a down-the-line backhand that might have missed fractionally, but no one bothered to argue.

As a receiver, he seemed bent on humiliation. He lobbed with undisguised enjoyment. His greatest delight was to wrong-foot an opponent. Another couple of games and I'd seen enough. Perkins was a near tournament-level player with a very nasty streak. His main weakness was a tendency to overaggression. He missed a smash that he should really have let bounce. His racket frame paid the penalty for that error. I played another two sets of mixed doubles, playing once against Doc. He hit some very good shots and was clearly enjoying himself. I did okay, didn't disgrace myself. I took my strip down after that game and told Doc I'd have to go when Perkins took off.

"I watched him," Doc said. "An A-type personality if ever I saw one."

I used my towel to wipe away the sweat. Last night's drinks had been well and truly metabolized. "Meaning?"

Doc smiled. "Asshole. Glad you got me out here, Cliff. I was in a rut. Take care of yourself, boy. I won't shake hands. I imagine you want to put on your cloak of darkness."

He laughed and walked away, swishing his racket. When he told me to take care of myself I knew what he meant. *Take care of my daughter.* Perkins was playing in a mixed set, concentrating his attack on the woman on the other side of the net. She happened to be the blonde I'd played with before, and she was standing up to him pretty well. I drifted off toward the members' parking lot, where there were a good many Volvos, Mercedes, and BMWs. No customized AP or BAR license plates to give me a hint. It came down, I decided, to the black Porsche or the red Alfa Romeo. I took a bet on the Porsche. Back at my car I wriggled out of my shorts and into a pair of jeans. I eased out of the damp tennis shirt, toweled off, and put on an old army shirt with a tail that hung down well over the holstered .38.

I was wrong about the car. Perkins zipped out in the red Alfa two cigarettes later. He seemed to be in a hurry, or perhaps he just drove that way. The tires squealed on the first turn, and he left some rubber on the road at the lights. Maybe that's what you have to do in a red Alfa. I wouldn't know. For all the showiness, it was easy to keep up with him. Driving speedway style between the lights in Sydney, you're lucky to make up any time at all on Grandpa out for his weekend spin. I followed him to Double Bay. It was hardly worth the drive. I was surprised he hadn't jogged it, but maybe the Alfa needed a run. He turned abruptly, barely signaling, and nosed up to the door of a garage, one of a set of eight that seemed to belong to a row of big houses with deep front gardens set up above the road. The garages appeared to be cut into the base of a ridge hill with the houses on the top.

I stopped on the other side of the road just a few meters farther and got out of my car quickly. Perkins had used a remote-control device to open the garage door. The Alfa slid inside, and I went after it into a kind of car cave—sandstone walls, cement floor, fluorescent light. Perkins didn't notice me until he was out of the car.

"What the hell d'you think you're doing?" He was all aggression off the court as well as on, quickly removing his sunglasses, raising one of his rackets threateningly.

"My name's Hardy. We have to talk."

He put the sunglasses on the roof of the car with his keys and the second racket. "You were at the courts. I saw you."

"High marks. You play a mean game."

He half-turned toward a door that led somewhere. A tunnel up to the houses? "If you don't leave immediately I'll call the police."

"What will you tell them about Virginia

Shaw and the bloke who took a shot at me a couple of hours after I called your office?"

He moved forward, gripping the racket. Not much of a weapon, but he was bigger than me and, I suppose, sure of himself, having just won three or four sets. "I don't know who you are or what you're raving about," he snarled. "But I'm warning you, get off my property before you get hurt."

I moved up too. "I don't like warnings, Andrew. I like to know what's going on."

The use of his first name annoyed and provoked him, as it was intended to do. He swung the racket at my head, but I'd been ready for that from the first, and I ducked under the swing and hit him with a short right jolt directly on the monogrammed pocket of his tennis shirt. A hard blow above the heart can paralyze anyone who isn't either trained to cope with it or so full of booze and rage it doesn't matter. Andrew, for all his flash, wasn't a boxer or a street fighter. He went down in a heap and lay gasping for wind and strength on the concrete floor. He tried to sit up, but his legs were like jelly and he fell, getting more oil stains on his tailored, sharkskin shorts.

I'd been wanting to hit someone for the

past few days and now I'd done it. Somehow, it didn't give me the satisfaction I'd expected. I looked down at him as he fought for his breath and dignity, and suddenly I had doubts. With the wind knocked out of him, his clothes dirty, and his pride hurt, he didn't seem so formidable. Also, he looked genuinely puzzled. He levered himself up on unsteady legs, gripped the car-door handle, and struggled upright.

"Who . . . who did you say you are?"

"Cliff Hardy. I'm a private detective."

"You behave like one. I'm calling the police if you don't leave immediately. I'm going to take some sort of action against you anyway."

He was starting to recover his no-doubt considerable confidence, and I was losing ground. He wasn't behaving as I'd expected. "I want to talk about Virginia Shaw. She's my client."

That got his attention but, perhaps understandably, he was more cautious than interested. "I'm not sure that I know anyone by that name."

"You know her, Perkins. You set her up

with Charles Meadowbank. She hired me to deliver you a message."

"You have a strange way of carrying out your commissions."

This wasn't going anything like the way it was supposed to. I was on the defensive now and he could see it. He massaged the place where I'd hit him, applied a little pressure, and winced. I reminded myself about the phone call to his office and the bullet whining off the bricks in St. Peters Lane. We were standing in the garage with the door open to the street. It wasn't the right place to conduct this sort of business, and I felt I had to get some leverage on him somehow. I pointed to his sports bag on the seat of the Alfa. "Collect your stuff and close the garage, then we'll step into your place and have a talk."

"Don't give me orders! You're trespassing, you're guilty of assault—"

I pushed him back against the car. "Listen, I was there when Meadowbank got shot. You're involved. Then someone took a shot at me. I'm holding you responsible until something convinces me otherwise."

He bent and picked up the racket that had bounced off the wall and lay near the front wheel of the car. I was half hoping he'd give it another try, but he didn't. He reached in for his bag and then shut the car door. He moved past me and touched a switch on the wall. The garage door slid into place on oiled tracks. "Very well," Perkins said. "I'll give you a few minutes, but your PEA license is hanging by a thread."

He opened the door at the back of the garage and we went up some steps to a path that led to the house. Perkins took the steps up to the front door three at a time until his bruised chest slowed him down. The massive front door was open. We stepped into a dim lobby.

Perkins started up the curving staircase that was about twice as wide as mine in Glebe and had no missing uprights. "I own the top two floors."

"Good for you. Anyone live with you?"

"Not at the moment, no."

He opened a door on the first level—entrance hall, carpet, high ceiling. I followed him into a sitting room half the size of a tennis court, with three doors to other rooms and one wall made entirely of glass. The view was toward the Royal Sydney golf course, with a lot of trees in between. Perkins put his sports bag and rackets down on a chair. The furniture was big and old, the carpet thick and oriental, the paintings big and modern. The room screamed money. Perkins stood in the middle of his carpet and said, "You wanted to talk—talk."

I shook my head. "Not here. I feel overwhelmed by your affluence. Where's the kitchen? I could do with a drink."

"Good idea." He went to the window and pressed a couple of buttons. Glass panels slid apart and warm air flowed into the stuffy room. Then he opened a door and we went down a short passage to a kitchen that looked as if it had been built in the last century but outfitted last year. It was all metal and glass, bristling with electrical appliances. The fridge was a double-door monster, and you could have roasted a sheep in the oven. Perkins washed his hands at the sink and dried them on a spotlessly white hand towel. "Of course, we could have had a drink in the den, but since you prefer the kitchen, what will you have?"

"Beer, if you've got it."

"Think so." He opened the fridge and rattled around inside it, coming up with two bottles of Heineken. It seemed to me that he'd taken longer about it and made more noise than was necessary, but I was too slow to react. I felt something metallic press into the base of my skull and then move away to the left.

"This thing behind your ear is a shotgun," a calm voice behind me said, "and you should stand very, very still."

9

I DID AS I WAS TOLD. PERKINS PUT THE beer on the kitchen table and let out a long breath.

"Thanks, Carl," he said.

"Okay, Mr. Perkins. What now?"

"I'm not sure."

I felt a hand move down my spine and then the gun being pulled from its holster. "Carrying a gun," Carl said.

"I've got a permit."

Perkins laughed, well in charge of the situation now, the way he liked to be. "It still extends my options, if you see what I mean."

I saw, and I didn't like it.

"The question is, do I call the police or let Carl deal with you out back . . . or do something else?"

He was a dangerous customer. I could see him almost tasting the violence, wondering how far he could go with it. All the way? Just possibly. Armed private detective breaks in, assaults prominent barrister, causing physical injury. I hadn't seen Carl yet, but he sounded capable and willing. It was one of those times when you have to do something to take the initiative, whatever the risk. I turned slowly, reached up, and moved the barrel of the shotgun, still without looking at Carl. I was eye-locked with Perkins.

"Don't make it worse than it is," I said. "Let's call it square for now. Where was the buzzer? In the garage or up here?"

"Both," Perkins said.

"Neat. You take all the points. We still have to talk. Tell Carl to put my gun in the fridge or somewhere and go away. You probably want that beer as much as I do."

Perkins was a quick decider. He nodded

and took a bottle opener from a hook on the wall. "It's all right, Carl. There won't be a problem."

"What about the gun, Mr. Perkins?"

"Unload it and leave it here."

Carl was a heavily built type with wide shoulders, not a candidate for the Meadowbank job. He leaned his shotgun against the fridge and expertly released the swing-out mechanism of the .38. He upended the gun, and the cartridges dropped into his hand. He put the gun and cartridges on top of the fridge, picked up his twelve-gauge, and left through a back door without speaking again.

"Man of few words," I said.

Perkins levered the tops from the bottles. "But of efficient action. He keeps watch on this set of houses twenty-four hours a day. Don't ask me how he does it."

"He doesn't. It's not possible. But if he's there when he's needed that's all it takes."

"Hmm." He handed me a bottle. We sat at the table and drank. Very convivial. Perkins had regained his composure and had his innate nastiness under control. He appeared to be thinking as he drank. He tore off a section of paper towel and wiped his mouth. "Something you said interested me."

"Virginia Shaw, I—"

"No, I may or may not talk about that matter. I haven't decided. You said you rang my office."

"Yesterday, about ten A.M."

"And spoke to whom?"

"A woman." I searched my memory. "Julie . . . Farnham?"

"Juliet Farquhar. And what was discussed?"

"Nothing much. I said I wanted to speak to you about Miss Shaw. She said you had no client by that name and that I should try some other Perkins. I said I wanted to talk to you anyway. I got the impression she consulted you. Then she said you'd be out of town on business for a while."

"You didn't believe her and you persisted?"

"After someone took a shot at me and yelled at me to stay out of the Meadowbank thing. Seemed to me you had to be behind that."

The beer was cold and good. We drank at about the same pace and I had the odd feeling that we were thinking at about the same pace and along the same lines. Perkins put his empty bottle down on the table and used the paper towel again. He had thick lips and a problem with keeping them dry. "I can appreciate the reason for your intrusion and aggression," he said. "But I wasn't in my office at that time yesterday, and Miss Farquhar didn't mention your call to me."

"And you do have a client named Virginia Shaw?"

"Not . . . officially."

"Would Miss Farquhar know about this unofficial client?"

"Until now, I would have thought not."

My turn to drain the bottle. I used the back of my hand to wipe my mouth. Perkins was looking more worried now than at any time so far. I had an advantage, but wasn't sure how to exploit it. When in doubt, go for the chain of command. "What's Miss Farquhar's job? How long has she been with you?"

Perkins frowned. A lot of horizontal wrinkles formed on his forehead below the red, crinkled waves of his hair—not a pretty sight. "A couple of months. She's my . . . legal secretary. She has a Bachelor of Jurisprudence degree from Monash."

"Meaning that she knows a lot about the law, but she's not a qualified practitioner and she's not doing articles?"

Perkins nodded. "She's a very capable young woman."

"Maybe too capable. There's something going on here. Virginia Shaw thinks that Charles Meadowbank was killed because he didn't want to go through with the divorce. You helped to set that divorce up."

"Not really," Perkins said. "I'm not acting for either party. I just did Charles a favor by putting him in touch with Virginia."

"You might have helped to get him killed."

"Don't say that! I don't understand any of this. How do I know you're telling the truth?"

"Call Juliet Farquhar. She's the link."

His hesitation spoke volumes. Perkins wasn't the sort of man who hesitated unnecessarily—he'd been caught off guard, and he didn't like it. Juliet Farquhar was coolly playing a game of her own, and he didn't want to think about what the consequences might be for him. I now had my strategy. "Don't piss around," I said. "Somebody's plans have gone badly wrong. Your Miss Farquhar could be getting you involved in something very nasty, or she could be in great danger herself. Maybe both."

Perkins stood up and grabbed the wall phone. He didn't need to refer to his little black book to get the number. He dialed rapidly. I opened the fridge, pulled out two more beers, and opened them. I took a drink and put the other bottle within Perkins's reach. He ignored it.

"No answer." He slammed the phone back into its housing.

I shrugged. "She could be anywhere."

Perkins shook his head and seized the bottle. "We were supposed to be going out tonight." He glanced at his watch. "Drinks at six. She'd be getting ready by now. She puts in a lot of time on her appearance."

I took another pull on the bottle and then pushed it away. Strong. I got up and took my gun and the bullets down from the fridge.

Perkins almost choked on his next hasty swig of Heineken. It was no way to drink high-quality beer. "What . . . what are you doing?"

I loaded the gun, trying not to make the action too melodramatic. "You'd better tell me where she lives, unless you want to come with me."

"I've been stupid," he said wearily. "She's a very exciting woman."

All of a sudden Andrew Perkins didn't look as impressive as he had on the tennis court and as he no doubt did in a courtroom. He ran his hand back over his head and feathered up his hair, which was thinner than it had first looked. It was receding at the sides too, something careful arrangement had concealed. I closed the cylinder and put the gun in its holster. The click of the mechanism made him twitch. I didn't like Perkins lording it over me, but I didn't want him coming to pieces either. At that moment I probably could have gotten a check for Virginia Shaw out of him and walked away, but it had gone beyond that. Below the wall phone there was a message pad with a ballpoint pen attached to it by a chain. I tore a leaf from the pad.

"Where does she live?"

Perkins had almost finished his second

bottle. "In Brontë, Barker Avenue, Number ten, Unit sixteen."

I wrote the information along with a description of the woman's car and Perkins's number on the slip. "You're her employer, maybe you should come with me."

He shook his head. "I'm more than that. She . . . knows things about me. If she's betrayed me . . . I . . . I have a violent temper. It's better I don't go."

"Suit yourself. Have you got a key?"

He went into the sitting room and came back with a leather key holder. He detached a key and handed it over. His compliance puzzled me.

I said, "I'm not acting in your interests, you understand."

He smiled and freckles stood out on his face, which had lost all color. "Exactly in whose interests *are* you acting, Hardy?"

"Will I have any trouble from Carl if I just walk out of here?"

Perkins shook his head.

"You stay put," I said. "You'll be hearing from me or the police or both."

He shrugged and tilted the beer bottle to his flabby, moist mouth.

* * *

I didn't see Carl, but I had a feeling he was watching me from somewhere and would have been on the job in a flash if I'd tried to steal the Alfa. Useful bloke, Carl. It wasn't far to Brontë and the roads weren't too busy. The exercise and the beer had given me a lift, and I'd recovered some of the ground I'd lost with Perkins. I quickly rolled a cigarette while waiting for a light and got it lit at the next stop. This was getting interesting. Miss Farquhar was playing some kind of game and I was keen to learn the rules from her. If she wasn't at home I'd just have to find her. It was one of the things I was supposed to be good at doing.

Unlike some avenues where there isn't a tree in sight, this one had plenty—plane trees and she-oaks on both sides as the road curved up away from the beach over what must originally have been a sandhill. Mostly blocks of flats, the occasional set of semis, and a few cottages. The flats I was looking for were set on a big block well back from the road. A lot of houses must have come down to provide the space. There were three modern, pale brick buildings with big windows, each containing a dozen or more units. I parked in the street and approached on foot. A wide driveway led to a series of parking bays and carports. The higher the rent, the better the car protection. Perkins had told me that Miss Farquhar drove a white Mini that still carried its black-and-white Victorian license plates. It was sitting in its uncovered space, locked, neatly parked.

The layout of the buildings was logical and well posted. Miss Farquhar's place was on the second level of the middle building. There was a bit of to and fro going on—people getting back from the beach, a man carrying two cases of beer, a young couple dressed up to party. No one looked at me as I entered and went up the stairs. I could hear music coming from one of the flats when the beer carrier opened his door. The sound shut off abruptly when the door closed. The walls and doors were thick. It was just as well that I had the key, because breaking in would have been a tricky job. The door was solid and the lock was modern and well-fitted. I knocked several times and got no response. I used the key and went in.

A woman was lying face down on the floor in the hall. When I opened the door it just cleared her outstretched fingers. She had clawed at the carpet in her death throes and was lying at a crazy angle with her legs splayed out. She wore a tight white dress with a high neck. I let the door close behind me and bent down. Her dark hair was drawn up into an elaborate arrangement on the top of her head, and she'd been shot once in the back of the neck, just below where the hair began.

10

MORE DEATH. TOO MUCH DEATH. I FELT AS if I had absolutely no control over my movements, feelings, and decisions. I was crouched over the body, locked there, with everything surging and washing around inside me. She was obviously young, slender, and scarcely formed, like the village children I'd seen in Malaya, caught in the cross fire. The combination of memory and harsh, present reality was too much. I reeled, reached for the wall to support myself. *Don't touch that! You'll leave sweaty prints as if you'd signed your name and added your date of birth and the color of your eyes.* I regained my balance and stayed there, poised over the lifeless body like a vulture deciding where to peck. A cramp was building slowly in my left leg. I let it build, enjoyed the mounting pain.

The soft buzz of the telephone probably stopped me from shouting and lunging for the door handle. The insistent noise came from inside the flat, past the awkwardly sprawled body. I uncurled and gasped as the cramp gripped and relented. I staggered toward the sound. The telephone was on a low table, just where the hallway let into a dim space that smelled of stale tobacco and alcohol and something else.

I lifted the receiver.

"Hello, hello . . ." It was Andrew Perkins's voice, and I was almost glad to hear it.

"Juliet? Juliet?"

"This is Hardy," I said. "Juliet's dead. She's been shot. I'm calling the police."

"Hardy! Don't—"

I hung up on him and dialed. While I waited I poked around in the flat. Juliet Farquhar had some expensive clothes and shoes, a collection of law books, and not much else. A few paid and unpaid bills in a drawer indicated that she hadn't been in Sydney very long. The flat was large and pleasant, with two bedrooms and a good balcony. It was very sparsely furnished. She had a six-month lease and had borrowed the bond money and some start-up capital from one Henry Farquhar, her father, who lived in Newtown. They'd drawn up an arrangement, signed by them both, whereby she was to pay him back in monthly installments. I made a note of his address. There was no sign of her handbag or anything else that might have carried the day-to-day things like makeup, cigarettes, keys, an appointment book.

The expected knock came on the door. I opened up and would have been flattened in the rush if I hadn't been well-braced. There must have been eight cops, arguing among themselves, but all eager to get at me. In my anger I shoved the first two back before I saw that they had drawn their sidearms. "The body's right here! D'you want to walk in over it?"

That quieted them down. I held the door open and they stared at the dead woman for a few seconds before doing some quick conferring. Most of them then backed away. A big sergeant put his pistol back in its holster and gave me his mess-with-me-and-you'll-be-sorry look. "Are you Hardy or Perkins?"

"Hardy."

"Okay. Have you got the key to this place?"

I'd instinctively put it in my shirt pocket. I handed it over and he put it in the lock. "Right. Back up inside, Mr. Hardy." Over his shoulder he said, "Come on, Sergeant. The rest of you, piss off and wait for the detectives."

I backed up, and the big sergeant and a smaller man of the same rank followed me, stepping carefully around the corpse.

"That's far enough. My name's Wren. I'm from the Bondi station. This is Sergeant Clark from Coogee. We got two separate calls to this address. Our information is that you are armed."

I reached up under the tail of my shirt and produced the .38.

"Easy," Clark said. "Why are you armed?"

"I'm working."

He took the gun from me, holding it by

the stubby barrel. He didn't seem to know what to do next. Wren was amused. "Have you got any identification?"

I pulled out my wallet and showed him my PEA license. It didn't make Clark any happier. He wanted to take the license folder, but he didn't want to have both hands full. He shot a doubtful look at Wren.

Wren sighed. "This is bullshit, Clarkey, and you know it. We'd better sit down and wait for the geniuses. Where's the kitchen? I could do with a glass of water."

"Better not touch anything," Clark said.

"I never saw a murder scene yet where anything that was found there led to a conviction. How about you, Hardy?"

I shrugged. "This is only my second one, Sergeant. I wouldn't know."

"I'm glad to see you're not a smart ass," Clark said. "I say we go outside and wait. Have you touched anything in here?"

"Not a thing," I said. "Shouldn't you sniff my gun to make sure it hasn't been fired?"

"I was wrong," Clark said. "You *are* a smart ass. Out!"

Wren didn't protest. He was older and

wearier, cared less. As he went past the body he said, "Good figure. Wonder what the face looks like."

We stood outside the flat. Clark propped the door open with his foot, making him look ridiculous, but neither Wren nor I nor the uniformed constable looking on smiled. Wren looked at the door of Flat 15. "Anyone home?" he asked the constable.

"Don't know, Sergeant."

"Try it, son. Try it."

There was no response to the constable's knock, but some voices carried up the stairs.

"Here they come," Wren said. He stamped his heavily shod feet. "I love the sound of detectives' shoe leather."

I was in big trouble, as Detective Coleman, the plainclothesman, explained to me at the Bondi station. Andrew Perkins was alleging trespass, assault, and coercion. According to him, I'd used force and threats to compel him to divulge the address of one of his employees and to surrender the key. Perkins had called the police emergency number, giving my description and describing me as dangerous. He had corroboration from a security man at his home.

"Carl," I said. "Picks his teeth with a shotgun. So what are you charging me with?"

"Depends. Mr. Perkins is receiving treatment for suspected fractured ribs. What do you have to say?"

"I phoned in about the dead woman."

"So you did. That's in your favor."

"You can't think I killed her. The blood was dry. She'd been dead for hours."

"An expert, are you, Hardy? You could have gone back to make things look different."

"Come on."

Coleman wasn't young and he wasn't keen. He knew the Homicide team would take the matter out of his hands. He was just going through the motions, but he had them down pat. "I like private detectives about as much as I like dogcatchers, Hardy," he said. "And I'm a dog lover. I'm tossing up whether to apply a little pressure on you. After all, I've got a prominent barrister as a complainant, and physical evidence."

"Like what?"

"Oh, a key, a firearm. We've had a look at it. Recently reloaded. Possibly recently fired."

"Bullshit."

"Careful, Hardy, you're out on a limb."

I had only one card to play and I played it. "Get in contact with a Darlinghurst detective named Gallagher, Ian Gallagher."

Coleman watched me roll a cigarette, my first assertive action since coming into his care. "You're one of this Gallagher's fizzes, are you?"

"No," I said. "But I'm only talking to him about this. I'm not talking to you."

The backhander he hit me with as he left the room had plenty of his weight and experience behind it. It hurt, rocked me back, tilted my chair, and I dropped my cigarette, but I judged I'd won the bout on points. I sat in the dreary room for an hour with nothing to do but smoke and think. Andrew Perkins had made a pretty smart move. With Juliet Farquhar dead, there was no support for my story that I'd phoned Perkins's office and been given the runaround. Virginia Shaw could be a problem for him, tying him into the Meadowbank killing, but he'd seemed genuinely puzzled by any such connection. He was covered and I was exposed.

It got cold down there below ground level. I was tired, thirsty, and hungry. *Gallagher, you bastard. Where are you?* After too many cigarettes, Coleman came back with a uniformed man. "Come on, Hardy," he said. "You're getting a visitor from Darlinghurst."

I stood up, collected my tobacco and lighter, and brushed away the cigarette ash. "About time."

"Yeah," Coleman said. "Detective Gallagher wasn't available just now. Detective Sergeant Colin Pascoe wants to have a word with you. He's on his way."

I slumped back down in the chair that suddenly felt very hard and uncomfortable. "What about a cup of coffee?"

"I'll see what I can do."

The coffee came a few minutes later, but it didn't do me much good. It was cold for one thing, and there was no sugar to put in it. I badly needed a lift. I also needed some ideas. I didn't like the notion of spilling my guts to Pascoe. His bull-at-a-gate methods would be likely to send Virginia Shaw running for cover and leave me facing serious charges from Andrew Perkins.

After another wait Coleman opened the door and ushered Pascoe in. Coleman hesitated, but Pascoe stared at him until the door closed and Coleman's footsteps retreated. Pascoe swaggered across the room, stepped behind me, and hit me with a rabbit punch on the back of the neck. I was tense, not ready for it, and the blow had a maximum effect. My head flopped forward, my feet slid, and I banged my nose on the table. Pascoe laughed. I gripped the edges of the table and levered myself back up into a sitting position. There was blood on my face and my shirt. It dripped onto the floor. I wiped at it with my hand and pushed the chair back in order to stand.

Pascoe's kick ripped the chair out from under me, and I fell heavily into the pool of blood. I tried to get up, slipped, and fell again. The next time I made it up, but Pascoe wasn't finished. He picked up the chair and jabbed me in the midsection with the back of it. I doubled up and he swore when some blood sprayed over him. Where the next punch hit me I don't know, but I was on the floor, by a wall, and he was standing over me.

"Now, what did you have to say to my little mate Gallagher that you didn't want to say to me?"

I concentrated on breathing and getting some leverage against the wall and didn't answer.

"You're like those fuckin' commo demonstrators, Hardy. You don't fight back." He kicked me lightly in the ribs.

I grabbed his foot the second it connected, jerked down, and twisted, getting a lot of torque on his knee. He yelled and flailed for balance. I let go and staggered up as he bent over to check the knee. I lowered my shoulder and bored in on him, hammering him back against the wall. Blood was flying from my face, spattering him. He was bellowing, pinned against the wall. I kneed him in the crotch and felt the wind go out of him. He was slumping forward, retching, in the perfect position for a head butt, and I wanted to spread his red-veined nose across his face. Adrenaline was rushing through me. I got set to do it.

The door hit the wall with a crash and the shout stopped me dead.

"Back off, you! Get back!"

I stepped away. Pascoe slid down the wall

until I thought he was going to hit the floor.
But he straightened, wincing as the weight
came on his knee. I wasn't in much better
shape myself, with a stiff neck, various aches
and pains, and blood still dripping from my
nose. A tall, thin man in a light gray suit had
come into the room with Coleman. He stood
quite still surveying the scene—overturned
chair, blood-spattered walls and floor, and two
men looking as if they'd gone fifteen hard
rounds.

The man in gray slapped the hat he was
carrying against his leg. "G'day, Col," he said.

Jesus, I thought. *They're mates. Maybe him
and Coleman'll hold me while Pascoe gets even.* I
checked my nose with my shirt sleeve. The
bleeding had slowed. I sniffed and moved farther away from Pascoe, keeping a wary eye on
the other two cops.

"Inspector," Pascoe said. He took out a
handkerchief and wiped his face. Then he
stumbled toward the table and leaned on it,
easing the damaged knee. I'd been more of a
boxer than a wrestler in my fighting youth, but
I'd done a good job on that knee.

The inspector righted the fallen chair and
examined it for blood before sitting on it.

"You're a silly bugger, Colin," he said. "This is a Homicide matter. You'd better go and clean yourself up."

"This cunt was trying to go behind my back."

"The way I saw it he was ready to do your head some serious damage. Piss off, Colin. You too, Roy. I want to have a few quiet words with Mr. Hardy here."

Coleman and Pascoe left the room, Pascoe hobbling perhaps a shade more than he needed to. I moved forward and got my tobacco and lighter from the table. Then I sat on the other chair and made a cigarette. When I'd finished, the cigarette had a little blood on it but I lit it just the same.

"I'm Bob Loggins, Homicide Squad. I'm investigating the Meadowbank killing. I'm a mate of Grant Evans."

I expelled the smoke in a long, relieved plume. The action made the point of my jaw on the right side ache, and I realized that was where Pascoe's punch had hit me. "Inspector," I said. "I'm very, very glad to meet you."

11

CHIEF INSPECTOR BOB LOGGINS WAS EV-
erything Coleman and Pascoe weren't—calm,
reasonable, personally secure. Of course, our
mutual friendship with Grant Evans helped,
but you need a little luck in this life. First, he
wanted to know what had provoked Pascoe's
violence. I told him and he clucked his
tongue.

"You might have expected that."

"I was hoping to get to Gallagher direct."

Loggins shook his head. "Col Pascoe's

been divorced twice with the third time coming up. His work's his life. You picked him as a fat, lazy slob?"

"Not exactly," I said. "Jaded."

"Well, you were right and wrong. I gather you're not one of these bleeding hearts who's got a defense attorney on tap—going to want photos taken of your bruises to bring a harassment case?"

I shook my head. "This is professional for me, Inspector, not political."

"Thank Christ for that. I could do with a drink. How about you?"

I stared at him. "I've got assault charges against me—trespass, coercion . . ."

Loggins returned the stare with cool, steady, pale gray eyes that matched his suit, hat, and everything else about him. "Bullshit," he said. "Andrew Perkins couldn't get the truth out past his fucking front teeth. Is it a deal? You walk out of here as sweet as a sunbeam and I buy you a drink?"

"Deal," I said.

Pascoe and Coleman kept well out of the way. I was shown to a washroom, and I cleaned myself up as best I could. Loggins located an old police shirt somewhere and I put it on. I had some blood on my jeans and my nose was puffy and red, but you see worse in Bondi every day. We left the station and walked to the Bondi Hotel. With his hat on his head, Loggins couldn't have been anything else but a cop. He told me he'd run me back to my car later and we could pick up my gun after we'd had a talk. This degree of cooperation made me a little suspicious. If he paid for the drinks I'd really wonder.

We settled down in the saloon bar with middies of old, got our cigarettes going, and I gave him an edited version of my recent activities. I held a few things back—like Virginia Shaw had feared for her life and left the city and I had a contact number for her. I made it sound like a straight line from her and her fee to Perkins and then via my phone call to the shot fired in St. Peters Lane and on to the discovery of Juliet Farquhar's body. Loggins listened in silence, smoking and sipping his beer. I was tired and feeling the wear and tear of the day by the time I finished. Loggins remained silent.

"That's about it, Inspector."

"Is that what you were going to tell Gallagher?"

"Pretty much. I was worried that Perkins was going to bring charges. I wanted someone on my side. Also, Gallagher seemed to think there was something tricky behind the Meadowbank killing. I thought he'd be interested."

"Thinks that, does he? What's he got in mind?"

I hesitated. There was nothing to prevent Loggins from dropping me straight back in the shit at the Bondi station if he felt that way. A policeman's promises are conditional on him getting what he wants. It wasn't smart to appear as if I'd shot my wad. "I think you'd better ask him, Inspector."

"I will, son. I will."

I took a chance. "You're investigating Meadowbank's murder, right? How is it looking?"

"No fucking good. No chance of this bloke at Perkins's place being the shooter?"

I shook my head. "Wrong build, everything wrong."

"How about the one who took a pop at you?"

"No way to know. I might know the voice if I heard it again, but I didn't see anyone."

Loggins drained his glass. "I wonder if he'll come after you again."

"Why should he? I don't know anything."

Loggins smiled. "That may be. But it might be possible to convey the impression that you know a lot."

"Jesus," I said. "I'm not sure . . ."

"Like earning a living, do you, Hardy?"

This was it—the price to be paid. "I've hardly started earning one in this game."

"You could do okay at it, with the right help and contacts. Or you could be back sniffing around burned-out factories and cars within the month."

"Shit."

"Don't get me wrong. I'm joking, more or less. Look, I think we should have a little conference—you, me, and Gallagher. Figure a few things out. What d'you say?"

"I'd say this must be a big case."

Loggins eased his chair back. "It is. Let's go and get your gun and your vehicle."

Technically, when I got home in my own car with my gun in its holster—all courtesy of Bob Loggins—I was late for my phone call to Melbourne. The twenty-four hours had been up for a while. I made the call anyway and got the same male voice.

"Hold on," it said.

I held. I had a glass of wine by the phone and a very full, very hot bath waiting for me and my bruises. My nose and jaw throbbed. I realized that I hadn't been this battered since the army, and before that when I'd boxed as an amateur, and before that . . . I was recalling school-ground fights with Mickey Fussell and Brian Hobbs when that man-pleasing voice came over the line: "Mr. Hardy? Mr. Hardy, this is Virginia Shaw. Why are you calling?"

Good question. I took a gulp of wine. *Hold the anger down, Cliff. Easy does it.* Easier said than done. The words came out in a rush. "A lot's been happening. I've seen Andrew Perkins. I've been shot at. A woman who works for Perkins is dead."

"I don't understand."

"Neither do I. Look, who's this guy who answers the phone? And would you mind telling me where you are?"

"I . . . I don't think that's a very good idea."

"I've had to talk to the police, Miss Shaw. Several times. It hasn't been much fun. I've been trying to keep you out of it as much as I can, but—"

"Yes. Oh, yes, please! Keep me out of it, Mr. Hardy. I'll pay you well."

"Payment's not the main issue. Have you ever heard of a woman named Juliet Farquhar?"

Five hundred miles apart and communicating over a wire, I could tell by the quality of the silence that she knew the name. "She's dead, Miss Shaw," I said roughly. "She was shot, possibly by the same man who shot your boyfriend."

"God. Oh, God."

She sounded very frightened. Also, she hadn't asked about getting her fee out of Perkins. Offering to pay me more and not very concerned about the money I was supposed to be bringing in. For someone in her business, that amounted to real fear. I let her stew in it for a moment. What the hell? She was underground in Melbourne with efficient-sounding protection. I was the one hanging my ass out in the warm Sydney wind.

"Miss Shaw," I said, "the police have got

me in a bit of a bind. They want to use me as some kind of a bait to get at Meadowbank's killer. I haven't got the details yet, but how does that sound to you?"

"That sounds very dangerous."

"I think so too. Now, I'm still trying to do a job for you, but you can understand that I feel very vulnerable. Do you follow me?"

A whisper. "Yes."

"I have the feeling that you're not a part of all this shit."

"I'm not! I'm not! I swear to you."

"I want to believe you, but you won't tell me where you are, who you're with, or anything else."

"I'm too afraid."

"So you didn't tell me anything like the whole story when we first met?"

"No. I'm sorry, but, no, I didn't. Everything I told you was true, absolutely true. But there's more. Much more, and I can't—"

"Okay. I think the police have got some idea of this. God knows what it is, I haven't got a clue. But I don't want to be their decoy, Miss Shaw . . . Miss Shaw?"

There was some kind of commotion at the other end—raised voices arguing. She sounded more resolved when she spoke again. "I understand. I hope the police are on the right track."

"So do I. Give me something. A name, a place, a hint, so I don't go into this thing totally blind. Something I can work with in both our interests."

I drank the rest of my wine, wanted a cigarette but didn't dare let go of the receiver to roll one. The pause seemed interminable. I'd gritted my teeth, and my jaw gave me pain. I probed with my tongue for a loose tooth.

"Dick Maxwell," she said. "He's in your business."

She hung up, but the buzzing on the dead line wasn't a completely unhopeful sound.

The phone rang as soon as I replaced it, and I picked it up with some annoyance—at this rate my bath was going to be ice cold. My injuries were stiffening up.

"Cliff, it's me. How are you?"

Cyn. I'd scarcely thought of her in the last twenty-four hours. "I'm okay, love. Been busy. How about you?"

"It's very exciting."

What is? I thought. "That's good. Are you

in Cairns? I didn't find out where you were staying."

"I didn't know for sure. I'm in a town house with one of the project people up here. I'll give you the number."

She did and I wrote it down. She chatted on about the job, making it sound more like one for a hydraulic engineer than an architect. I made some stock responses, not really interested.

"Cliff, are you in trouble? You sound strange."

"Well, private detecting's a bit different from company work," I said. "More demanding."

"Look, the weather's great up here. Why don't you come up when you finish what you're doing? I assume you're getting paid."

Always the sting in the tail with Cyn. "Would you like that, love?"

"It'd be great. You'd like it here."

I had my doubts about that. I'd pretty much stayed away from the tropics after Malaya—too many bad memories of bullets and jungle and teeming rain—but this offer sounded good. I said so and we talked amiably for a few minutes before she remembered that her host would be paying for the call.

"Reverse the charges next time," I said.

"Good night, Cliff. Take care."

You bet I will, starting on Monday. Loggins had scheduled a meeting for Tuesday morning, when he expected to have comparative ballistics reports on the Meadowbank and Farquhar murders and other information. I'd agreed to the meeting, not having much option. Loggins was confident that Gallagher would attend. I wondered whether any pressure would be put on him in the meantime. I hoped I hadn't dumped Gallagher in it. I already had one sworn enemy in the Darlinghurst detective division; raising it to two would probably mean shutting up shop.

I ran some more water into the bath and let myself down slowly into the comforting warmth. Cyn and I had taken a bath together on the first night after we'd moved into the house. We were both exhausted after throwing out several decades worth of rubbish, including innumerable layers of linoleum. A few floorboards had come up with the bottom layer. But the hot water had worked okay and we'd had some fun in the bath and upstairs on a mattress afterward. Pretty good memories, and maybe things hadn't gone too sour between us even now. I lay there until the water got cool. Then I put on a terry-cloth bathrobe and made myself some Welsh rarebit with lashings of Worcestershire sauce. It was close to midnight when I sat down to eat after a day of tennis, two-way assault and battery, and sudden, brutal death.

12

SUNDAYS WERE QUIET IN GLEBE. THE CON-
tainer terminal across the water was silent, and
the traffic rumble was absent. The planes were
fewer and came later. My neighbors didn't
bang doors and start engines at ungodly hours,
and Glebe was not lawn mower territory. As a
result of all this silence and stillness, and my
exertions of the day before, I slept late. It was
an unusually peaceful sleep, and I felt fine after some coffee and a toasted bacon sandwich.

I didn't look as good as I felt. My nose

was swollen to nearly twice its size, and it wasn't a small hooter to begin with. At least it hadn't been broken again. Twice was quite enough. One eye was slightly blackened, but sunglasses would conceal that. My jaw was a bit puffy, but it had stopped aching. On balance, I'd hurt Pascoe more than he'd hurt me, and that was only physically. When it came to pride, I was miles ahead—although that could pose problems for later on. But it was a fine, clear morning, and I was a temporary bachelor with no responsibilities and some interesting work at hand.

I drank some more coffee out in the concrete backyard and thought about flying up to Cairns to spend some time in the sun with Cyn. Maybe Loggins's idea of acting as bait was the quickest way to get through to that happy scenario. Somehow, I wasn't able to convince myself. The phone rang and it was Doc Lee on the line, chirping cheerfully and asking me how my Sam Spade act had worked. He sounded very uppish—maybe he'd felt rejuvenated by the tennis and had slipped it to Inge for the first time in a while.

"It went okay, Doc," I said. "Thanks for the help."

"I asked around a bit about that Perkins chap. Discreetly, you understand. You need to watch your step with him, boy."

"I know. I spoke to Cyn last night. She's enjoying the job. I might go up and see her in a week or so."

"Good idea. I'm glad to hear you two are getting along. Inge sends her best."

All sweetness and light on the home front. A rare condition. I turned my mind to the weighty question of locating a private investigator by the name of Dick—presumably Richard—Maxwell. There was no telephone listing for him, but that wasn't too deflating. His agency might have a name, like Ace Detective, or he might work for one of the big shows like the Montalban Agency or the Blaine outfit. A few security firms employ private eyes too, and there are some attached to big hotels. I needed firsthand information, and the obvious source was Ernie Glass. The problem was that the easiest place to find Ernie, the Tottenham Hotel on Glebe Point Road, was closed because it was Sunday. Easiest? It was the only place I'd ever talked with him. I knew he lived in the immediate vicinity of the pub, and the only thing to do was to wander down there. The Tottenham did a steady sly grog trade on Sunday, selling bottles and flagons after midday in the backyard at double the weekday price. Maximum of three bottles and one flagon to a customer. Ernie always laid in stocks; I'd seen him toting them carefully away on a Saturday evening. An ant. But one of the Sunday grasshoppers would be sure to know where he lived.

The rear entrance to the Tottenham was in a lane quite a long way back from the main road. The business was conducted discreetly, with a minimum of noise and fuss. The police knew about it, of course, and occasionally moved in to close the operation down for a few weeks. Token stuff. They either got a kickback or decided the peace was better kept by allowing drinkers to get their poison than by depriving them. Cynics accepted the first motive, idealists the second. I tended to think it was probably a bit of both.

Things were quiet this Sunday. I wandered up and down after having a word with, and passing a few dollars to, Freddy, the lookout. The customers varied between winos after their port and muscatel and better-heeled types who'd forgotten to lay in the Riesling for lunch. Ernie's mates weren't of either stamp—army pals, old jockeys, footballers and boxers, and women of the world who liked a drink and a joke. I knew a few of them by sight and I'd asked Freddy, who worked as a bartender and bouncer at the pub, to give me a nod if one of Ernie's friends showed up.

It was warm in the lane and I was ready for a drink myself by the time Freddy called me over. The man he indicated was middle-aged, with a seamed face and a thick body that might once have been athletic.

"Reg, this is Cliff Hardy. He's a mate of Ernie Glass's. Reg Kerr, Cliff. Reg used to play for Balmain. Winger."

I shook Reg's hand and tried not to look shocked at the realization that he was short a few fingers.

"Yeah," he drawled. "Just couldn't catch the fuckin' thing after I lost them digits."

He had three bottles of Resch's pilsner in a paper bag under his arm. "Party?" I asked.

He winked. "Couple of ladies coming by. Could be. Well, nice to meet you, Cliff."

"You need more than three bottles for a party," I said. "Freddy, you could organize another three, couldn't you?"

"Sure," Freddy said. He took the note I gave him, looked both ways up and down the lane, and went through the back gate into the pub's yard.

"I'm looking for Ernie, Reg," I said. "I don't have his address. I only ever met him here. D'you happen to know where he lives?"

"Not a cop, are you? Ernie's a bit behind on the child support, I hear."

"No. I'm in the same game—private investigation."

He laughed. "And you can't find him. You blokes are full of shit."

I grinned. "It's Sunday. The usual channels are closed."

Freddy came back with the bottles and my change and then took up his post down the lane. I stuffed the money in a pocket and offered the paper bag to Reg. "What do you say? I could find him tomorrow, but I need him today. It's important."

"Say you know him?"

"Yes. He helped me get into the business."

"Who does he support?"

Fair enough question in the context, but football wasn't one of my passions and I couldn't recall ever having a conversation about it with Ernie. Then it came to me, his outrage when his club's try had been declared invalid and the other side had won a finals match.

"Newtown," I said.

"Right. The cunt. Ernie's got a flat in Ferry Road. Flat two, four A. Say I said hello. Ta for the beer."

I thanked him, gave Freddy the thumbs-up, and began to thread my way through the back streets. No time like the present. Ferry Road follows the lie of the land, running down to Blackwattle Bay. The area is undergoing a lot of change—rusty, ramshackle factories coming down, small boatyards and workshops closing, apartment buildings rising on the sites. There are still some of the old houses, narrow one- and two-story terraces, jammed close together with built-in verandas and porches dating back to the Depression when rentable space was at a premium. Number 4A was smarter than most—a well-maintained terrace with two mailboxes on the gate, indicating that it was divided into only two flats.

Flat 2 was reached by an iron staircase running up the side of the building to a balcony at the back. I knocked at the glass-paneled door, and Ernie's distinctive shape appeared in the mottled pane almost immediately. Ernie stood about six four when he was younger, but had stooped a bit in recent years. He was still big all over—shoulders, arms, and chest. He pushed his glasses back from the end of his big nose.

"Cliff, old son. What brings you around here? Don't tell me your wife's left you and you need someone to find her?"

"Ha, ha. No, mate, I need a line on one of our coworkers. I get the feeling he's more your vintage than mine."

That's the way it went with Ernie and me—light jabs and counters. He ushered me through open double doors into the living room. The flat was laid out unconventionally, with the living and sleeping quarters at the back and the kitchen and bathroom in the front. The reason was obvious—a wide-angle view from the balcony of Blackwattle Bay. I sat in a deep leather armchair while Ernie went to the kitchen. He came back with a bottle of beer and two glasses.

"Any chance of a sandwich, Ernie?"

"Jesus, doesn't that good-looking wife of yours feed you?"

I accepted the glass and took a pull. "Thanks. She's away up north on a job. I can feed myself, but I've been hanging around the Tottenham trying to find out your address."

"Yeah, well, I don't advertise it. Hang on."

Away he lumbered again, coming back this time with a plate carrying a bread roll, a lump of cheese, a tomato, and a knife. "Go for it. What happened to your nose?"

I got busy with the knife. "A copper clobbered me."

"What did I tell you about getting along with the police?"

"It's all right," I said, chewing. "Another cop came to my rescue."

Ernie shook his head. "Cliff, Cliff, I hope you know what you're doing. I told you to make friends with some cops, not depend on them or trust them. This didn't happen around here or I'd have heard."

Ernie is a slow, deliberate talker. I'd eaten most of the roll by the time he finished. "No, mate. Eastern suburbs. I think I can stay on top of it, but I need to talk to a private eye named Richard Maxwell to help me do that. D'you know him?"

He reached for his glass, drained it, and filled us up again. Ernie usually drinks the way he talks, as if there's no rush. Maxwell's name seemed to have speeded him up a bit. "I know Dick Maxwell. I wish I didn't."

"Why's that?"

"He's a pisspot Pommy poofter, that's why. Don't have anything to do with him, Cliff. He'd sell his sister and his mother just a split second before he'd sell his brother and his father."

"I have to talk to him, Ernie. It's about a divorce case—"

"That's about all he ever does, the bastard. How he keeps his license I'll never know. He must have an in with somebody."

"Shit, that's an angle I haven't considered."

"With Maxwell, there's bound to be a slew of angles you haven't figured. Do you want to tell me about it?"

I finished the food and beer before answering in order to give myself time to think. "To be honest, Ernie," I said, "I think it'd be better for you if I didn't. My feeling is that this is pretty bloody dangerous. Look, I'll get in touch if I need any hands-on help. I'm still trying to manage it the way you said."

"Remind me."

"With brains rather than blows."

"Okay. Last I heard he was in a drying-out joint in Heathcote."

"Heathcote."

"Yeah, bit of a hike to the nearest pub, I understand. Fresh air, all that. He must be in a very bad way to go there. Fresh air and lemonade—Maxwell's not used to them, they might kill him. Never heard of him taking the cure before, but I suppose there's a first time for everything."

"How recent's this information, Ernie? And how good is it?"

His thick, salt-and-pepper eyebrows lifted. "Don't get cheeky with me, young Hardy. The information's fresh and I think it's good because I came upon it by accident."

I knew what he meant and didn't press him. You hear lies all the time; you're more likely to *overhear* the truth. He gave me the name of the clinic and his own phone number and didn't ask any more questions about the job, so we had accorded each other a mutual respect. I refused more beer, thanked him for the help and the calories, and stood up. I was anxious to get moving. I was also anxious to get outside and have a smoke. Ernie is a passionate antismoker, and to light up in his home would be like smoking in church. We shook hands at the door.

I had a last question. "What does he look like?"

"Medium-sized, getting fat. Pale. Always wears a hat. He's got this little gingery toothbrush mustache. No muscle on him. You're a lot tougher than Maxwell, Cliff," he said. "But I'm not sure you're smarter, and smarter usually wins."

"Thanks, Ernie. I'll work on it."

13

HEATHCOTE WAS WELL OFF MY USUAL
beat. I knew you drove down the Princes
Highway to get to it, and that was about all. I
walked home slowly, sucking on a cigarette
and speculating about what I might learn from
Richard Maxwell. Something about divorce. It
didn't sound too promising. I wondered what I
could use for leverage on Maxwell, apart from
the obvious thing. I rejected the idea for most
of the walk, but had accepted it by the time I
reached the house.

Inside, I checked the street maps and found that Heathcote was past Engadine and consisted of two clusters of streets on either side of the highway, both bordered by national park. The clinic was on Goburra Road, on the right coming from the city and one of the last marked roads before the suburb gave way to park land and the meandering Heathcote Creek. It was hard to tell from the map and I didn't know the area, but it was a fair bet that the nearest liquor outlet would be at a distance only a desperate man would walk.

Ernie had said Maxwell was smart. He'd also indicated where he was vulnerable. I found an unopened bottle of gin in a cupboard and tossed it from hand to hand. I didn't like the idea of tempting a drunk, but it was my safety and career on the line and, apart from Cyn and a couple of friendships, there weren't too many things more important than those. I put the bottle in a soft leather briefcase along with my .38 and a manila folder containing some blank sheets of paper. I had one of Alistair Menzies's cards in my shirt pocket. I debated whether to call the clinic first, but decided against it. I had some money, a brief-

case, and Menzies's card. If they weren't
enough, I had the gun.

The drive south out of Sydney was not the
prettiest—too many used-car lots, auto-parts
stores, and drive-in liquor stores. The land-
scape had been blasted by the internal-com-
bustion engine. By Kogarah Bay, other forces
such as wind and water took over, and Tom
Ugly's Bridge was a nice reminder of a quieter
time. Mind you, it was dull back then before
the European migrants and TV and mass advertising arrived, and perhaps the noise and
dirt were the prices we had to pay for more
interesting lives. That was Cyn's opinion anyway, her usual rejoinder when I got nostalgic
about the taste of bottled beer and fish and
chips in newspaper and fight night at Rushcut-
ters Bay stadium.

I turned off the highway and drove
through the winding streets of Heathcote. The
farther from the main road they were, the narrower and rougher they got. Goburra Road was
a wide, unpaved track with a few established
houses on one side and a few more in the process of being built. The national park began

on the other side, low scrub that deepened into dense bush in the near distance. I drove slowly with the windows down, avoiding the ruts. There was some dust from the road, but the smell of the trees and the bird noises compensated. After the gas-fume monotony of the highway it was a nice change.

The King A. Hartwell Clinic was a big white stucco building, three or four stories with two wings. At a guess, as an architect's husband who lived with books full of pictures of buildings, I'd say the place was put up around the time of the first World War, when Heathcote was really out in the sticks. The clinic, therefore, was a little island of freehold or leasehold on the edge of a very big chunk of land owned by the crown. Interesting. The grounds looked to run to about five acres, well-watered with plenty of lawns, flower beds, and trees. Healthful and restful. I wouldn't have minded a short stay there myself, judging from outside appearances.

I drove through two imposing gateposts—one of which carried a big brass plaque bearing the name of the clinic—and up a curving gravel drive. I parked where a sign said VISI-TORS. I was the only one. There were a dozen or so cars, ordinary Holdens, Fords, VWs, and a couple of sleek, well-polished jobs, parked in space marked STAFF. I did up a few buttons on my sports shirt, tugged at it to reduce the wrinkles, and stuck my briefcase under my arm. I closed the windows and locked the car. A few people strolling on the grounds looked up at the noise of the slamming door. The place was extraordinarily quiet. The strollers strolled on, and I walked toward the sandstone steps leading up to a heavy door, standing wide open.

The lobby was cool and quiet. Behind a reception desk a woman wearing a stylized version of a nurse's cap was working at an electric typewriter that was almost noiseless. The place had more the feel of a hotel than a hospital. There were pigeonholes with keys hanging from them, some with mail tucked inside. The pictures on the walls were bright, landscapes mostly, and there was a big, three-dimensional model of the clinic and its grounds set out in a glass case. A wide cedar staircase ascended from the lobby, and the entrance to the ground level was through a set of double doors. When I felt I'd absorbed everything useful, I coughed to announce my arrival.

The woman looked up and favored me with a smile. Maybe I'd smile more if I had teeth like hers. "Can I help you, sir?"

I approached the desk, unzipping my briefcase and letting the edges of the papers show. I took out a Menzies card and handed it to her. She was standing now, a tall, slim woman wearing a white dress with a blue belt and a touch of blue at the neck and sleeves—nurse-like. She looked at the card and then at me.

"Mr. Menzies—"

"No, no. My name is Vernon Morris. I'm an associate of Mr. Menzies. I'd like to have a word with Mr. Richard Maxwell, if I may. Legal matter. Won't take a minute."

She frowned. "You should have telephoned."

"I did. On Friday. There should be a note of it. It's a bit off the beaten track here, isn't it? And this was the best time for someone from our office to come. I'm on my way back from some work in Maianbar, you see, so it wasn't too far out of the way. I was assured . . ."

She searched through the bits and pieces on the desk, opening and closing folders and slapping at piles of paper. A corkboard with notices pinned to it, positioned handy to the telephone, yielded nothing. I craned forward, peering at the pigeonholes. They were tagged with initials. There was an RM, all right, but the letters weren't unusual. Who knows? It could have been Roger Miller.

"I'm sorry. There's nothing here."

I plucked at the papers. "It'll only take a minute. Perhaps you could ask Mr. Maxwell?"

A new look came over her face—skeptical, defensive. She appeared to be a person whose natural bent was cooperation but who'd learned to act differently, and I could see her registering and assessing details now—the battered nose, the creased clothes. "I'm not confirming that there is anyone of that name here," she said. "Do you understand?"

"No, I don't understand."

It was only a slight movement and she did it well, but I knew what it meant and I looked automatically toward the double doors. Sure enough, they opened, and a very big man in a white coverall came out. A tailored coverall, with zippers and well-cut trousers. He was well-cut and well-groomed himself, with a body builder's chest and shoulders and that tapered look they have. In my experience they taper both ways—physically from the thighs down and mentally from the mouth up. This one had the conventional bleached-blond good looks marred by a bad case of adolescent acne scarring. He probably wore pancake makeup when he competed.

"Yes, Mrs. Tomlinson?" he said.

So far he was well within his field of competence.

"This gentleman has no appointment and refuses to leave, Mr. Matthews."

"I'm here on legitimate business," I said.

Matthews wore white tennis shoes, and he came forward quickly and quietly. So far, no voices had been raised, no discordant sounds made. The King A. Hartwell Clinic was very big on quiet.

"I think you should leave," Matthews said. He covered the last stretch very quickly and his big hand was on my shoulder, gripping hard.

"I want to see someone in authority here."

A quick nod from Mrs. Tomlinson, and

Matthews went into action. He was good. He spun me around 180 degrees, literally. A well-balanced, very strong man can do that to a lighter one. Before I knew it, I was being marched through the door and down the steps. Matthews was an expert manhandler. He changed his grip, altered the pressure, kept me guessing as to where the force would be applied next. To someone with no experience of hand-to-hand fighting it would have been totally intimidating. I trotted along, pretending to be just such a person. My dust-streaked Falcon stood alone in the VISITORS space like a UFO, and Matthews steered me unerringly toward it.

He was enjoying himself. Some men are happy with pumping up their muscles, flexing them for admiring audiences, striving for yet more definition. Not Matthews. He wanted to use his strength against less strong men. A nasty trait, compensating for something. I let him frog-march me around to the driver's side, so that the car body was between us and the clinic. I fumbled in the briefcase as if searching for the ignition key. Matthews's wide blue eyes went even wider when I brought the Smith & Wesson out and jammed the muzzle up into his left nostril. For intimidation, the great advantage of a revolver is that you can cock it one-handed with the trigger action. *Click, click.* Sheer terror.

I felt the big man's strength ebb away as he looked into my face. "You've had your fun, Matthews," I said. "Now prop yourself back against the car and be very careful. I don't like gymnasium cowboys heavying me."

"Just doing my job," he said. He moved back. All the force had gone out of him. We both knew he could do things quickly, but not quicker than a finger can pull a trigger.

"Your job's changed. You're going to have to show a bit of initiative."

"How . . . how do you mean?"

I kept the .38 nestled inside his nose and reached back for my credentials. "I'm a private investigator. My name's Hardy. I want to talk to Dick Maxwell. Just talk. Let your eyes wander over this."

I showed him the license inside its plastic cover. Apparently he could read, but he didn't say anything.

"You can remember your routines, can't you? Press this, snatch that, repetitions, all that shit?"

"Yeah."

"Okay. I want you to remember a few things. Tell Maxwell I found out where he was through Ernie Glass. Got that? Ernie Glass."

"Ernie Glass."

"Good. I don't have any beef with him that I know of. My client is Virginia Shaw. Who?"

"Virginia Shaw."

"Right." I took the gun away and Matthews started to relax. I moved back a step, released the breech, and spilled the shells slowly into my hand. Matthews stared at me as if I were mad. I handed him the bullets and put the gun on the hood of the car. I flicked the breech closed and had a solid weapon in my hand—not a deadly one, but Matthews knew what it could do to his classic profile. He looked down at the bullets clustered in his big, calloused paw.

"Tell Maxwell I want to talk. That's all. You've got the shells. I can't harm him. I'll wait here for ten minutes. If he doesn't show I'll leave, but tell him this: If I go away without seeing him, the news of where he is travels all over Sydney, starting from when I get to a phone. Have you got that?"

Matthews nodded. He turned and walked toward the clinic. I knew he wanted to get things back on the old basis between us, with him grabbing and twisting things, but he was bright enough to understand that this wasn't a matter of pecs and lats and half nelsons.

14

I LEANED BACK AGAINST THE CAR, KEEP-
ing well clear of the revolver, and rolled a cigarette. Everything felt wrong about the King A.
Hartwell Clinic. Summoning the muscle when
I'd done nothing more than be a bit insistent
was an overreaction. And Matthews wasn't
there to lift drunks in and out of bed. I studied
the place as I smoked, keeping an eye out for
flanking movements. The people walking in
the gardens could well have been dipsomani-
acs drying out. They walked slowly, as if they

had a lot of time, too much time, which is a feeling that oppresses alcoholics when they're not drinking. So I've been told. A couple of them could have been visiting husbands or wives, except that there were no cars in the visitors' spaces except mine.

Through a tall stand of trees I caught a glint that could have been a swimming pool. Nothing inappropriate about that. Hydrotherapy. The place looked perfect. It just felt wrong. I finished the cigarette and was beginning to think my tactic hadn't worked when I saw a man coming down the steps from the south wing. He wore a cream suit, and as soon as he reached ground level and stepped out into the sun, he carefully placed a panama hat on his head. Then he put on sunglasses. Then he took out a gold cigarette case and lit up. I waited for him to wipe his face with a silk handkerchief and shoot his cuffs, but he didn't. He strolled toward me, one hand holding his cigarette, the other in his jacket pocket.

Not that there was much doubt about it, but the ginger bristle on his top lip confirmed his identity. He stopped about twenty feet away and took a small automatic from his pocket. His big pink hand, with a large signet ring on one finger, concealed most of the gun, which he pointed at my middle shirt button.

"Well," he said. "Tall, dark, and not very handsome. What the fuck do you want?"

"You can put the gun away, Dick. I just want to talk."

He smiled. His teeth were tobacco-stained and uneven. He had a blotchy, damp-looking complexion. "I dislike the word 'dick' except as an affectionate term for the male organ."

His accent was BBC English, grown a little lazy. He lifted his cigarette and puffed theatrically. His gun hand was fairly steady, but he was beginning to find the pose—or standing in the sun—a strain. I was under some strain myself. I've had too much to do with guns to like them, and I don't particularly care to have them pointed at me. I eased away slowly from the car and looked around. There was a bench under a tree twenty yards away.

I pointed. "We could go over there and sit in the shade. This sun can't be good for a man in your condition."

He licked his thin lips. He had a cold sore, cracked and angry-looking, just below the mustache on the left side. "You're absolutely right, dear boy. You toddle over first, and don't you dare go near that pistol."

"It's empty."

"So you say."

We walked into the patch of shade. I sat down at one end of the bench and put the briefcase on the grass beside me. Maxwell undid his double-breasted jacket and fanned himself with his hat before he sat at the other end. He was almost completely bald, and with the jacket open I could see his belly straining at the band of his trousers. He wore a tailored shirt with a long, peaked collar and a paisley cravat. He'd finished his cigarette. He still had the gun. "Show me your miserable credentials."

I passed them across. He glanced down, sniffed, and threw the folder back. "A license to starve or prosper, depending on how you use it."

"I haven't been at it long."

"You say you know Ernest Glass?"

"I know him well. He told me you were here. He said he stumbled on the information by accident. I gather you don't want people to know you're here. That's why you're talking to me now."

"Very acute." He probed with his tongue at the cold sore. Suddenly, he put the gun away and took off his sunglasses. His eyes were red and he rubbed them redder. Then he lit another cigarette and drew on it deeply. He coughed.

"Is this really a drying-out tank?" I asked.

"It performs other functions. A bolt-hole, you might call it. But yes, God damn it. I'm taking the cure. Tea, fruit juice, and coffee. Coffee, fruit juice, and tea. It's making me ill. My body chemistry's all awry."

"Why're you here, Maxwell? What are you afraid of? What's your involvement with Virginia Shaw?"

He threw back his head and laughed. It was a rich, melodious sound, but practiced rather than genuine. I was beginning to doubt Ernie's assessment of Maxwell's intelligence —he seemed like a set of poses and mannerisms with nothing behind them. "You *do* like to ask the right questions, don't you, Hardy?"

"Saves time," I said. "You know about Charles Meadowbank getting shot, I assume. Did you know that a woman who worked for

Andrew Perkins was killed too? Someone also took a shot at me. I'm thought to know things I don't know."

"Better you shouldn't."

"Wrong. Better I should. The police are looking to use me as bait, or a beater, or whatever the hell you pheasant shooters want to call it."

Maxwell laughed again, but this time with a less theatrical note. "That's all an act, dear boy. I'm from South London. Pick any gutter you like. I've lived on this accent and my wits for forty years."

"Ernie Glass said you were smart. I must say I can't see much sign of it—holing up in a drunk tank, dry as a day-old dog turd, and jumping at shadows."

"Glass is all right. I'm alarmed that he knows I'm here though."

"Don't worry," I improvised. "I'll hear from him if anyone else inquires. And I've asked him to keep quiet about where you are."

"Good, good." Maxwell took off his hat and fanned himself again. He made it look natural, but I was ready for something like that. Out of the corner of my eye I saw Matthews pull back from a position he'd moved to about fifty yards away.

"If I seem a little slow-witted, Hardy, it's because this enforced abstinence is causing my brain to seize up. You're quite right, of course. I'm in hiding here. I . . ."

I opened the brief case, took out the gin bottle, and unscrewed the cap. "It's warm and there's no tonic, ice, or slices of lemon."

He eyed the bottle like a desert traveler stumbling across an oasis. "You're utterly unscrupulous. I *have* been trying."

"I don't give a shit," I said. "Your weaknesses are your problem. I want information because my life's in danger, and I believe this one's all I've got. Oil your brains and talk to me. Maybe I can even help you."

The last remark tipped the balance. Maybe it just enabled him to rationalize his action. He grabbed the bottle, swiveled a little to shield himself from view, and tilted it to his mouth. He swallowed deeply twice before I took it away from him.

"Oh my God, that's better. Christ, I wish I could be sure I could trust you."

"If you were sure it wouldn't be trust. It'd be something else."

He shot me a surprised look. "Having a drink yourself?"

Warm, neat gin wasn't my drink of choice, even if the lip of the bottle hadn't touched his cold sore. "No," I said. "Tell me what's going on and you can take the rest back to your cell."

He looked glum. "They search you when you've been in contact with a civilian. I'll have to drink it here and smoke like mad and chew gum. Give me another pull, and I'll tell you what I can. I don't know everything, not by a long shot, and I don't want to."

I handed him the bottle. He took a long drink and used his hat again to signal to Matthews. He didn't bother to conceal the action this time. Out came the cigarette case and lighter, and he got himself set. He told me that some prominent Sydney identities were involved in a conspiracy to get themselves trouble-free, reputation-saving divorces. Charles Meadowbank was one, and he named two others—Bruce Redding, who was a member of Parliament, and a surgeon named Molesworth. He said there were more, possibly bigger people, whose names he didn't know.

"My belief is," he said, "that a certain amount of wife swapping has been going on in high places. Now these people want to make the swaps permanent, but they don't want fuss or the precious names of their various intendeds to be sullied."

I said it sounded like a difficult thing to organize. He agreed, but said it had been done through the help of several lawyers like Perkins, a number of women like Virginia Shaw, and several private investigators like himself.

"Perkins claimed to know nothing about the Meadowbank killing. It looked as if this woman who worked for him had some involvement. She's the one who was killed."

"He probably used her as a front and she exceeded her instructions. This whole thing has got out of hand."

"He seemed genuinely shocked when he learned of her murder."

Maxwell shrugged and put his cigarette stub under the heel of his pale suede shoe. He glanced at the outline of the bottle in my bag, then looked away. "Like me, he probably had some involvement, but hadn't expected things to take the turn they did."

"What exactly was your involvement?"

"I helped to set up the women to be core-spondents in the Redding and Molesworth matters. There was a sort of pool of money, a fighting fund established from these lucrative clients, and I was well paid. I'm using those funds here now. There was a promise of more when the divorces all went through."

That dried him out and I had to give him another go at the bottle to get the flow started. "Don't get pissed on me," I said. "It won't work."

"There's not enough here to do that. I had an enormous lunch out of sheer boredom. My stomach is well-lined."

I rolled a cigarette and listened as he told me of his alarm when he heard, first, that Meadowbank was pulling out of the agreement, and then that he had been shot. "That was all a bit too sticky for me, old boy. I decided it was best to get out of town and lie low for a spell. I was very perturbed when you turned up, to put it mildly. But I must say you had a brilliant strategy for winning my trust."

The liquor was making him more confi-dent now, and oily. I hadn't liked him to begin with and the dislike was growing, but I had a lot more to learn. "There must be someone behind all this then," I said. "Someone holding it all together."

He lit another cigarette and didn't speak.

"That's what I need to know. That name."

He shook his head. "I simply don't know. I took instructions by telephone."

"Come on."

"It's true. Of course, I sniffed around a little and came up with Andrew Perkins's name, and another member of our noble profession was in on it too. I'm reluctant to name him, and I'm sure he knows no more than I do. He's a timid soul as well and might have gone underground. There's a good deal of surmise in what I'm telling you, Hardy. I have to admit that."

I felt rather let down. Maxwell's sketch of what lay behind the deaths and deceptions Virginia Shaw had involved me in was interesting and convincing, as far as it went. But without a name, something to follow up, it all began to feel as fragile as a used tissue. I let my disappointment show by zipping up the bag. "This isn't enough, *Dicky*. I'm considering hauling you out of here by the scruff of the neck."

Maxwell shifted toward me on the seat; his soft hand shot out and fondled the bottle. "Don't do that. Matthews would certainly stop you. He's armed this time and he's a very vindictive type. I'll be honest with you. I can't swear I'd give you that name if I knew it. There's a lot of power and money behind this thing. But I don't know it. Give me another drink."

"Why the hell should I? What can I do with what you've told me? One of the cops I'm in touch with *knows* there's something going on. Maybe he'll be interested to get a few more clues, but that's not going to get me off the hook. I could ask the police to come and question you, I suppose."

He sniffed, and his tongue licked at the cracked cold sore. "If the impression I leave with is that you're going to send the police here, I'll be off within the hour. I assure you. Give me a bloody drink. Can't you see I'm working myself up to tell you something more?"

He was sweating. Beads of moisture had formed where his hatband met his bald head, and they were threatening to run down into his eyes. He dabbed at the spot with a moist hand. His breath carried to me across the short distance between us—sweet from the gin but going sour, tainted with tobacco and fear. I gave him the bottle. He'd drunk about half of the contents, and he disposed of another sizable slug. I looked around and saw Matthews leaning against a tree. He was stripping a twig and crushing the leaves before dropping them to the ground. I was anxious to get away from the place.

"Okay. You've had your drink. Let's hear it."

He drew in a deep breath and surrendered the bottle. I let the last couple of inches run out onto the ground and he watched, almost approvingly. I'd seen it before. *Now* he'd go on the wagon! Like hell he would.

"If you keep me altogether out of it, I'll tell you who shot Charles Meadowbank," he said.

15

I WAS BACK ON THE HIGHWAY BEFORE THE thought struck me that Richard Maxwell might have outsmarted me the way Ernie had predicted. What did I have? A name and a few vague allegations about some prominent people, who were well-protected from the likes of me. Maxwell could be on his way north or south at that very moment. Somehow, I didn't think so. He was a very frightened man, past his best and losing his grip. God knows what he would have done when he and his liver were younger and fitter. But as it was, he'd backed me. I was almost flattered.

Lawrence "Chalky" Teacher. The name was familiar, but not too familiar. If Maxwell had simply nominated one of the well-known thugs about town, I would have had my suspicions. But Chalky Teacher was a more dubious and shadowy figure. I'd heard of him for years, as an associate of criminals, a probable police informer, and a man to be careful of. But as I approached Rockdale and got the first glimpse of the city skyline, I realized that I had no idea of what Teacher was like physically—big, small, or in-between. And I couldn't connect him with a single event, organization, or individual. I couldn't recall reading about him in the tabloids or hearing a reference to him on television. It was all word-of-mouth stuff, rumor and innuendo.

I had some thinking to do, and the hot inside of a not very comfortable car, with my shirt sticking to my back and my head aching from the roughhousing of yesterday and the tension of today, wasn't the place to do it. I needed a cool, shady beer garden, with Nina Simone playing in the background and ice tinkling in a double scotch. It was Sunday, and the nearest thing to that was thirty miles away, outside the metropolitan area. The Balmain-Rozelle RSL Club wouldn't do, and I didn't want to go home to the empty house. I found myself turning off the highway and taking the road to Sydenham and then to Petersham.

Going to visit an old girlfriend in the condition I was in was a risky move. I knew it, but after the distasteful Maxwell I was in need of congenial human contact. Besides, Joan Dare was a journalist and might know something about Chalky Teacher. If she told me he was six feet three in his socks, I'd have a simple choice to make—go along with Loggins's plan to use me as bait or catch the next flight to Cairns.

Joan's house overlooks Petersham Park. It's a double-fronted cottage, freestanding with a deep backyard. Joan is a passionate gardener, and she bought the place because of the space. I jackhammered up hundreds of square feet of concrete for her during our brief affair, which took place while Cyn and I were having one of our separations a few years back. I knew Joan had plans for a prizewinning garden; I'd promised to haul the topsoil. Then

Cyn came back and it was over between Joan and me.

Someone else had carried the topsoil. When I pulled up outside the house I had trouble recognizing it. In two years the concrete wasteland had been turned into a small jungle. Creepers grew all over the front fence and twined around a pergola between the gate and the veranda. The green-painted concrete slabs in the front yard had been replaced by small-leafed ground cover, flower beds, and vines growing out of tubs. I could see shrubs and small palm trees growing along the side of the house and something bushier and taller sticking up at the back. The colors were reds and greens and white, and in the late afternoon the garden was humming with insects. The place reminded you of how quickly the whole six hundred square miles of Sydney would revert back to bush if it was allowed to.

I rang the front doorbell, but there was no answer. I wasn't discouraged. Joan didn't sit inside on fine days. I went around the side of the house, pushing my way through fronds and leaves and noting the new paint job on the clapboards, new plumbing, wiring, the works. Joan earned good money as the editor of the

"City Life" section of the *Sydney News*, and her only vices were red wine and her garden. I found her working on a terraced part of the steeply sloping backyard. She was wearing shorts, tennis shoes, and something with red and white spots tied around her chest. It made a thin stripe across her narrow back, suggesting that it was worn more for comfort than concealment.

"Joan."

She turned slowly, digging tool in hand. She wore neither sunglasses nor hat and had to shield her eyes against the low sun.

She said, "Who's that?" and I experienced a jolt, remembering her poor eyesight and her husky, intense voice.

"It's Cliff Hardy, Joan."

She straightened up to her full five feet six. She was as lean as I remembered, very tanned with short blond hair. Thin features, pointed face. She's a few years younger than me and had worn better. She dropped the trowel, pulled off her gardening gloves, and wiped sweat from her face as she edged closer. "So it is. Looking like a truck just hit him. Has she pissed off again, Cliff? That it?"

"No, Joan," I said. "I just wanted to see

you. Have a drink and maybe pick your brains. I've gone into the private eye game."

"I heard."

"The garden looks . . . amazing."

She snorted. "What would you know? You can't tell a bougainvillea from a banksia."

"I busted up the concrete."

"So you did. How could I forget? You drank a can of beer for every square foot."

I laughed. "It was bloody hard work. How are you, Joanie?"

"I'm good." She brushed her hands together. "Well, I was about to knock off anyway. I've got a couple of bottles of rosé chilled. How's that sound?"

"Great."

She stepped quickly forward and kissed me on the cheek. "Don't be so stiff. I'm over you a long time, sport. It's good to see you."

There was a wooden garden set on some flagstones near the back of the house under another pergola. Ferns hung in baskets from the cross beams, and creepers trailed around the uprights. I plunked myself down in one of the chairs and rolled a smoke while Joan went inside. A shower ran very briefly—Joan was one of the few women I'd ever known to take quick showers—and then she was back, carrying a bottle and two stemmed glasses. She'd changed into a long flower-patterned skirt and pale blue T-shirt. Her small, pointed breasts moved as she opened the wine. She poured two glasses full, another attractive habit of hers, and sank into a chair with a sigh. From the accuracy of her pouring I knew she'd put in her contact lenses. Without them, when it came to close work, anything was possible. She once told me she liked to garden without them and that when she surveyed what she'd done the effect was like looking at an impressionist painting. Then she'd put them in and get the details right.

"Cheers. It *does* look pretty good, doesn't it?"

I drank some of the cold, slightly spicy wine. "It looks terrific. Is it finished?"

She laughed. "That's what you have to understand about a garden. It's *never* finished. It's never over. And it never lets you down."

"Joan, I—"

"Forget it. We were both in the mood at the same time. You got out of the mood first, that's all. It would have been me a bit later.

Roll me one of those filthy fags of yours and tell me all about it."

I made her a cigarette, lit it, and talked for about ten minutes. She smoked, drank her wine, and listened. I could tell from her expression and nods that she knew about Meadowbank, had heard of Andrew Perkins, and that the name Bob Loggins wasn't unknown to her. I toned a few things down, didn't tell about Loggins's scheme, and left out Richard Maxwell's name. When I got to the politician and the doctor, Redding and Molesworth, her interest really picked up.

"Bruce Redding," she said, "and Dr. Leo Molesworth. Well, well."

"I've heard of Redding. He's a cabinet minister, isn't he? Who's Molesworth?"

"Redding's a junior minister, not actually in the cabinet but getting there. Molesworth's what they call a fashionable Macquarie Street surgeon. He's a hip-replacement man for the rich."

"Both with good motives for arranging quiet, smooth divorces?"

"Redding, certainly. Big Catholic population in his electorate. Molesworth, I'm not so sure about. Do society doctors have to watch their p's and q's? I wouldn't have thought so. Your informant suggested there were others involved?"

"Yep, apart from Meadowbank. I didn't get their names though."

Joan poured the last of the bottle and accepted another cigarette. I was feeling a lot better, considerably cooled down externally and internally, and relaxed by her calm, intelligent manner. I was confident that Joan would come up with something to help, but suddenly I remembered how I had sheltered Ernie Glass. I'd been careless, let my tongue run away with me, and told Joan very much more than I intended, and I felt guilty.

"Look, Joanie," I said, "this is dangerous stuff. I didn't mean to spill it all quite like this. I wanted some help with something specific."

She puffed smoke at me and laughed. "Big deal. I've got bigger secrets than this inside my head, *Mister* Hardy. And I've got the journalist's protection, remember? If I get pushed too hard I can publish."

"Not if you're dead, you can't."

"True. It *does* sound like pretty heavy stuff, and I've got a feeling there's more than a batch of easy divorces behind it, wouldn't you say?"

"Yeah, but what?"

"I can do some work on it. Discreetly. Redding won't be hard to sniff around. The good doctor's a bit trickier, but there're ways. Don't look so worried, Cliff. This is my business. You're doing me a favor by putting me on to it."

"You didn't see that girl dead in her flat."

"I've seen 'em. Now, something specific?"

I drank the rest of my wine and considered what to say. I was imbued with the idea that men protected women, even though I'd met plenty of women who needed no protection from anyone—I'd been shot at by women in Malaya. It was an idea that belonged in mothballs along with cardigans and tea parties and the nonworking wife. My own wife was working a thousand miles away, and I'd already told Joan almost as much as I knew. Still, it was a hard idea to shake, and I hesitated.

"You're pissing me off, Cliff," Joan said. "You know who hauled all these flagstones in here? Me. I've hitchhiked all over this country and Europe and Asia. I've got a thirty-two Beretta inside, and I'll take you on at target-shooting any day."

"The specific thing is Chalky Teacher."

"Jesus, how is he involved?"

"My information is that he killed Meadowbank."

"How did your informant come to know this?"

"He wouldn't tell me. Can you describe Teacher physically?"

She closed her eyes and leaned back. Her throat was a long, slim brown column, and the skin around her jaw and neck was taut. "I've seen him once or twice. He's a small man. Not more than five six. About my size, actually. Light build. He used to be a boxer. What's the division above the one Lionel Rose was in?"

"Rose was a bantam. The next one up's featherweight."

"That's it. He was an amateur featherweight boxer. He's not a featherweight criminal though."

"So I gather. How would I go about finding him? Do you know where he drinks? Who he hangs around with?"

"He doesn't drink. I know that much. I

don't know about the rest of it offhand, but I suppose I could find out if I made a few calls. Bit hard on Sunday though. How urgent is it?"

"Very. You sound reluctant."

"Now it's me who's worried on your behalf, Cliff. Teacher is very bad news. You mustn't even think of going up against him on your own. I won't help you do that. And if you start asking around about him in the pubs and so on, you'll find yourself in big trouble."

She got out another bottle of wine, and we talked about it for a while as we lowered the level. Eventually I agreed to go to Gallagher with whatever I got before confronting Teacher. It had been in my mind to do something like this anyway.

"Promise?" Joan said.

"I promise."

"Who is this Gallagher?"

"He's a detective at Darlinghurst. Bit younger than some, bright, ambitious. There seems to be a bit of subtlety about him."

"All right. I'll call a few people tonight. Might have something for you later or in the morning."

I thanked her and stood up to leave. She got up as well and we were standing there, only a foot apart, both with a fair bit of wine inside us and conspiratorially involved. I put my hands on her shoulders.

She stiffened. "Where is she, Cliff? Cyn."

"She's in Queensland on a job."

"How're things between you?"

"So-so."

"Work on it." She lifted my hands off, leaned forward, and pecked me on the cheek. I wanted more and reached for her, but she stepped away quickly. The better part of a bottle of wine hadn't slowed her down.

"Not a good idea," she said. "In fact, a very bad idea. Let's keep this on a business footing. If something publishable comes out of it, I've got the inside track, right?"

I picked up my tobacco and lighter. "Sure. Of course."

"Don't sulk, Cliff. You'll be glad when you get home. Let me tell you something. You know when this garden really started to grow properly?"

I shook my head. She took my arm and guided me toward the path down the side of the house. "When I finally got over the bloke after you."

16

JOAN DIDN'T CALL UNTIL AROUND EIGHT
thirty the following morning. I'd slept badly
and was edgy, wondering if she'd drawn a
blank or changed her mind. I snatched up the
phone.

"Hardy."

"Don't say it like a battle cry. This is
Joan. I've got a line on your man. Do I have
your promise you'll contact that cop as soon as
I've told you?"

"Sorry, Joan. Yes, I'll do that."

"Right. Well, Teacher's around, that's the first thing. Wouldn't help you much if he'd been in New Zealand for the last six months, would it? He's a hard man to pin down though —lives mostly in hotels and 'with friends,' if you get the idea. The last address I could get was one forty-three Botany Street, Coogee, but I'm told that he's not often there."

I wrote the address in my notebook. "Where is he often?"

"Your grammar's lousy. He works for a bookie named Max Wilton. The word is Max is into a few other things as well and needs someone like Chalky by his side. Wilton lives in Coogee too. Tonier address, number ten Hoadley Street. Said to be quite a pad."

"Is he often there?"

"Better. Yes, and he's often at the track riding horses and picking up information for Wilton and also in Centennial Park, jogging, and at the Bondi baths, swimming."

"Where does he lift weights and practice his fencing? When does he get time to read?"

"It's no joke, Cliff. A couple of the people I spoke to sounded very scared of him, and they aren't wimps themselves."

"Okay. That's great, Joanie. Just one

thing: Was there mention of an association between Teacher and any private detectives?"

"I don't think so. No, I'm sure there wasn't, but something rings a bell in that connection."

"What?"

"I can't place it. I'll let you know if it comes to me. Give me your office number."

I did, and she hung up after urging caution again. She didn't make a point of it, but I knew I was greatly in her debt. The sort of information she'd given me wasn't easily teased out. Some head-kickers, collectors, henchmen strut around the town like they own it, and they can be found by anyone, anytime, especially by journalists and cops. Characters like Teacher played it differently, preferring to keep their heads down and operate on the quiet. Joan must have called in some favors and given some undertakings to get the dope. I hoped I'd be able to keep my promises to her. I showered and shaved. My nose had returned almost to its normal crooked shape and my other aches and pains had eased. I made a pot of coffee, rolled my first Drum of the day, and called Detective Ian Gallagher.

"Gallagher here."

"It's Hardy. Can you talk?"

"Christ, Hardy. Yeah, for a minute, but Pascoe could be back any sec. What the fuck have you been doing?"

"Has Bob Loggins been in touch with you?"

"Yeah. Supposed to be some big meeting with you tomorrow."

"I have to see you before that. Today. Where and when?"

"Can't you give me some idea of what's going on?"

"What has Loggins told you?"

"Bugger all. I'm seeing him later today. Pascoe's shitting himself and I don't blame him. Loggins carries a lot of weight."

"Is he straight?"

"Jesus, what a question. Yes, as far as I know. Where are you now?"

"I'm in Glebe, but I'm on my way to my office in St. Peters Lane. Can you meet me there in an hour? You've got the address from the other night."

"An hour. Might be a bit more, but I'll be there. I hope you know what you're doing."

"Me too."

* * *

I parked out back behind the building that houses the tattoo parlor and went in to strike a deal with Primo Tomasetti. He put down his buzzing needle when I entered and told the client, a blond American marine corporal in a freshly laundered uniform, to take a breather.

"What's that mean?" the Yank said.

"A spell, a break, take five."

"Sure. Okay." The marine took out a pack of Chesterfields and lit up. He wasn't much over twenty, but he had the wary, old look jungle fighting gives a man. He was having "Mary, Mom, and Idaho" tattooed on his upper left arm inside a heart. Primo had the drawing on the table beside the needle and ink capsules. He'd gotten as far as "Mary" and "Mom."

"So, Cliff," Primo said. "You gonna drip oil all over my cement slab?"

"Five bucks a week," I said.

"Fifteen."

"Eight."

"Twelve."

"Ten."

"Okay, you've got a deal."

"And a key to this building."

"No problem."

I put a ten-dollar bill on the table and went past the client to a door opening out to a passage that led to a walkway running along the back of the row of buildings.

"Private eye," I heard Primo say.

"No kiddin'?" the Yank said. Then the needle started buzzing again.

I walked through to my building, up two flights of stairs, and along to my office. All quiet, as usual. No blondes, brunettes, or redheads in seamed stockings leaning against the door. The only thing attached to the door was the filing card on which I'd printed "Cliff Hardy, Private Investigator" and fastened with a thumb tack. Not quite as required by the Commercial Agents, etc., Act, but doing the job. Monday's mail had yet to arrive. I felt a slight sensation of achievement in getting Gallagher to agree to come here. After the last few days I'd seen enough of the inside of police stations. Maybe you could communicate differently with policemen on civilian ground. I hoped so. It was a punt, talking to Gallagher, but I sensed, along with the ambition, a maverick spirit in him, an impatience with bureaucracy and procedure that might work to my advantage. *Had* to work.

I heard him on the stairs soon after I'd rolled a supply of three cigarettes. I didn't want to press my luck, so I opened the door and waited for him. He came briskly along the corridor—no hat, jacket unbuttoned, tie slid down, at ease. He was carrying two foam cups with lids.

"I'll swear I saw a rat on the stairs," he said.

"That'd be Jack," I said. "I heard him squeak. He lets me know when any coppers come around."

He laughed and went past me into the office. He put the cups down on my desk and clicked his fingers. *"Due cappuccini,"* he said. "I live in Leichhardt."

I closed the door. "Good for you, Ian. I'm glad you could make it."

He lifted the lids from the cups, dropped them into the wastebasket, and took several packets of sugar and two plastic spoons from his pocket. "Somehow, Cliff," he said, "I got the feeling that there wouldn't be a lot of amenities around here."

"I've got a flagon of red in the drawer.

But it's just a shade early for a Glebe boy. I dunno about Leichhardt."

He put two packets of sugar into his coffee and stirred vigorously. I took mine without. We sipped and I lit a cigarette. He glanced around the room observing the decor, which you could have called shabby-functional.

"You should have something on the wall," he said. "Your medals, army commission, PEA license, something like that."

"I was thinking more of a dartboard."

The coffee had lost a bit too much of its heat. I kept drinking slowly while I tried to think fast, but Gallagher drained his cup. He began chopping into the plastic with his fingernails. I almost wished he'd bitten them. "Okay, Cliff, tell me why I'm here."

"Loggins wants to use me as bait to draw out whoever killed Meadowbank and the girl. His idea is to put it around that I know a lot and that I like to talk."

"Sounds like a good strategy."

"I don't care for it, so I've been doing some digging on my own. I've come up with a few things that I wanted to try on you."

"You want to waltz around with me, leaving Bob Loggins out of it? Loggins? I've already got my immediate superior hating my guts, I don't need one of the top Homicide detectives joining the club. I don't think I can help you."

It was what I expected and hoped he'd say. To jump straight at what I was offering you'd have to be crazy, and a crazy ally is worse than none at all. Still, I hoped to work on his vanity and ambition.

"I think you were on the right track," I said. "My information is that there's a conspiracy behind the two killings. It involves divorces, reputations, careers, probably property settlements as well. I've only got a few chips off the tip of the iceberg, but they're interesting."

Gallagher's young-old face set into lines of intense concentration. "Go on."

"I've got two names—Redding and Molesworth. I'm told there're more from the same side of the street. Redding you'd have heard of; Molesworth's a big-time surgeon. Meadowbank was in on it too. As I hear it, a couple of lawyers and PEAs arranged for convenient corespondents, permitting clean divorces. Andrew Perkins was in on it to some extent, but it looks as if Juliet Farquhar who worked in his office took her own run at it and became a nuisance. Meadowbank wanted to pull out. He'd got less interested in divorce. There's a possibility that whoever killed him really meant to get Virginia Shaw, or perhaps both of them. I'm not sure about that."

"Where have you been getting this?"

"Some from Virginia Shaw. I'm working for her now, in a way."

Gallagher seemed about to react to that, but he held off and continued to demolish his plastic cup. He had a lot of options to consider, and I didn't mind him taking his time.

"I've got another source too. Can't tell you who it is, but he's put the finger on the man who killed Meadowbank."

Gallagher's fair head with its carefully combed thick hair came up slowly. He dropped the cup and the bits he'd torn from it into the bin. "And who would that be?"

I shook my head. "I need some undertakings first."

"That's an unfortunate choice of words," Gallagher said. "But how about this: I go to Loggins now and tell him what you've told me. It fleshes out some things I had an inkling about. Then we haul you in and squeeze you until you cough up the name of this source of yours *and* the alleged killer and anything else we choose to ask you about. Col Pascoe's got a fucking truckload of charges he'd like to stick up you, don't forget."

"Wouldn't work."

"Why not?"

"First, you'd have to explain to Loggins how you went to me without talking to him first. That'd be hard, and Pascoe'd love it. Suppose you got past that somehow. I'd deny everything. Then you'd be in the possession of information with no way of accounting for it convincingly. It would have to occur to Loggins and Pascoe that you'd been talking to people you shouldn't, and without keeping a record. I'd be in the shit, sure, but you'd be in it with me, Ian."

He flashed the Redford grin. "Pretty smart. Okay, why don't you take the information to Loggins?"

"I don't trust him. I've got this nasty suspicion that what some Homicide detectives are best at is arranging homicides."

"That bespeaks a shocking want of confidence in the police force. Not that I'm saying the organization's perfect, mind. I've got a law degree from the University of New South Wales, did you know that?"

"I had the feeling you didn't go straight from your school certificate into the academy."

"Right. It's held me back in the force, the LL fucking B. Isn't that amazing? So, Cliff, you don't trust Pascoe because he's a nong, and you distrust Loggins because he's a Homicide squad heavy, but you do trust me?"

"No, I don't, but you're in the same boat as me, approximately. People are trying to use and manipulate you and you don't like it. Same here. Our interests sort of intersect on this."

Gallagher nodded. "You wanted undertakings. Like what?"

"Not much. I want to know everything Loggins says when you see him today."

Gallagher laughed. "Call that not much, do you? That's my fucking job, right there. What do I get in return?"

"The name of the killer and the chance to get hold of him and give him a shake while he's not expecting anything. Tonight."

"Alleged killer."

"An awful lot of things about him fit. I saw him, remember."

"Such as?"

"Uh uh," I said. "All that comes later."

Gallagher stood up. I noticed for the first time that his suit was an expensive piece of tailoring and fitted him very well. He didn't fiddle with cuffs or creases though. "Okay, Hardy," he said. "I'll be back at five this afternoon. I see Bob Loggins at three. Right now I've got a time sheet to falsify."

He gave me a businesslike nod and stalked toward the door. When he opened it I fancied I heard a noise outside, but it was probably only Jack the rat.

17

I RANG THE CAIRNS NUMBER CYN HAD
given me, but the person who answered told
me that Ms. Lee was spending the whole day
at the site. I left the message that Ms. Lee's
husband had called and would call again. Cyn
had kept her maiden name for professional
use. She joked that if we had a son we should
call him Lee Hardy. I suggested adding Pro-
prietary Limited, but she didn't seem to think
that was funny. Having children wasn't a subject that came up often, and when it did, my

reaction was almost always to make a joke of it. The thought of having a son chilled me. How can you teach someone to behave properly when you don't know how to behave yourself?

I answered the phone a few times through the day. Work was coming in. I lined up interviews for later in the week, explaining that I had a job on hand that was taking all my time, but I would be free soon. The prospective clients were promising: a missing-person case—not a child, thank God—and a Double Bay restaurateur who doubted the honesty of his partner. Sounded as if there could be a free meal or two in that one, but first I had to stay alive and in business. I went out and had a slice of pizza and a coffee for lunch, in keeping with my resolve to make it a dry day. The Falcon was sitting nicely on Primo's slab and only dripping a tiny amount of oil.

I bought a paper, which occupied a very small part of the afternoon. I knew that upcoming divorces had to be listed somewhere, possibly for public notice. But I didn't know where. I was acutely conscious of being new at the game. Ernie Glass had told me that a private investigator needed a "tame" cop—it seemed to me that a tame lawyer, auto mechanic, and dentist would come in handy too. I was trying not to admit it, but a tooth in the vicinity of where Coleman's backhander had landed was sending out signals. I puzzled about the keeping of notes. It didn't seem wise to make a record of my conversations with Maxwell and Joan Dare, and exactly where would I file them anyway? They didn't really belong under "Meadowbank" or "Shaw," and I wasn't desperate enough to open a file called "Survival." I blew dust from the office set of street maps and looked up the addresses for Teacher and his boss, Max Wilton. Joan said something about the name nagging at her, and I had the same feeling, as if there was a connection to be made between various bits of information. It eluded me though.

I smoked too much and was thinking seriously about a drop of red to ease the rough throat when the phone rang at about four thirty. Temptation put aside, I answered it.

"Hardy? This is Bob Loggins. I want to see you at College Street at ten sharp tomorrow morning. Okay?"

"How did the ballistics work out?"

"Ten o'clock. On the dot." He hung up. He was short on charm, long on confidence that I'd do what he wanted.

The phone rang again soon after. It was Gallagher this time, sounding tense and worried. He told me to meet him in a park on Norton Street in Leichhardt in half an hour.

"I thought you were coming here."

"I changed my mind. You be there, Hardy. I've gone out on a limb for you. You better have something good for me."

It was my day for being ordered around by coppers. I said I'd be there. I took the .38 out of its drawer, checked it over, and strapped it on. Before I left I took a quick one from the cask. They call Leichhardt "Little Italy," and when in Rome . . .

It took me longer than half an hour to get to the park, but I didn't mind keeping Gallagher waiting—no sense letting him have things all his own way. The traffic crawled along Parramatta Road, and I had to wait three cycles of the lights before getting around at Norton Street. The Italian flavor was struggling to get through the Australian ingredients, but a few of the restaurants had tables placed outside and many of the businesses had signs up in both local languages. The post office and town hall are solid pieces of Victoriana, like the pubs, but there was no such thing as a *pasticceria* in grandma's day. Cyn and I occasionally ate in Leichhardt, always at my bidding. She once said she thought I'd be happy with a dish consisting of pasta in red wine. Cyn's preference was for the kind of French cuisine that left me wondering if the tablecloth might be edible.

I like suburban parks, and the Pioneer memorial in Leichhardt was a beauty. It had all the essential features—a militaristic arch and a memorial stone listing the names of the municipality's fallen residents in two World Wars, an acre or so of grass with cement paths through it, and a few battling flower beds. The trees and shrubs either weren't really trying or didn't get enough water, and the white smudges on the grass indicated where dogs liked to shit. The backyards of Leichhardt were typically small and cemented over. The dog owners had to have somewhere for nature to take its course. My familiarity with the park stemmed from a few hours I'd spent in it after a fight with Cyn in a nearby restaurant. She walked out. I took the remainder of the Moyston claret to the park and absorbed alcohol, tobacco, and the atmosphere.

I parked alongside the adjacent high school and entered the park from the eastern side, near the bus terminal. People were strolling and sitting; the dog lovers were indulgently watching their charges sniff at tree trunks and garbage-can support posts. I was comforted by the sight of every one of them, the long and the short and the tall. The Hardys, Pettigrews, Flanagans, and Fanous— my antecedents—have been in Sydney for a long time. A Fanou—or a Le Fanou, as my sister Tess prefers it—was shot dead by the constabulary in The Rocks in the early 1860s. He was a publican, although Tess insists he was also a police undercover agent. Whatever the truth of that, I had no wish to emulate him, and the best protection against a police shooting, accidental or otherwise, is the presence of solid citizens.

I did a careful visual survey of the park. I didn't see any suspicious featherweights or heavies like Carl or Matthews. I realized how edgy I was and tried to force myself to calm down. Gallagher was sitting on a bench near the arch reading a newspaper. He did it well. It was his precinct; maybe he sat there and read the paper when he wasn't conspiring against his fellow officers. There were another couple of hours of daylight left, and I felt reasonably safe from direct attack. As I approached him I watched the street for cruising cars. I walked straight past Gallagher and did another lap of the park, looking, checking, trying to register any change in the configuration of things. People came and went—old men, kids. A bus stopped, dropped off some passengers and picked up others. I saw nothing to alarm me.

"You're careful, Hardy," Gallagher said. "That's good. I like that."

I sat on the bench beside him, fished out the makings, and made a cigarette. "Your good opinion is all I crave."

"Don't get smart. This was all your idea, remember."

"You approached me when I left the station, remember."

"What is this? Are you getting cold feet?"

I lit the cigarette and puffed smoke toward the memorial to the fallen. "No. Loggins called me just before you did. He wants to see me tomorrow morning."

"Right."

"What's on his mind?"

Gallagher rolled up his newspaper into the shape of a baton. He held it in his right hand and thumped it against his left palm. He gave it a solid whack, more the street copper's thump than the demonstrative gesture of the attorney. "You don't get a word out of me until you give me that name. Who killed Meadowbank, Hardy? According to your un-named source?"

It was put-up time and I knew it. I took a deep drag on the cigarette and let the words out slowly with the smoke. "Lawrence 'Chalky' Teacher," I said. "Ever heard of him?"

The noise Gallagher made was hard to interpret. It was something between a sigh and a grunt. "Chalky Teacher, yeah, I know him."

"My information is that he's the enforcer. The only other thing I know is that there might be another private investigator or two in on it. You see why I want to deal with the police?"

"Yes. And what do you want to do about it?"

"Get hold of Teacher and shake him. Maybe get some evidence—the gun, the stocking mask, something that ties him to Juliet Farquhar and this whole business. At worst, scare him, rattle him. See what happens."

Gallagher looked pained. "I can't do that."

"Why not?"

"I have to go through channels. Get a warrant, that means see a magistrate, that means clear it with Pascoe."

"You can't be serious. D'you mean you never picked up a known criminal on suspicion of something or other and gave him a hard time? Come on."

"And what would you be doing?"

"I'll back you up."

"If anything went wrong—anything—it'd mean my job. It's not worth the risk."

"I'm disappointed in you, Ian. I thought you wanted to cut the red tape and get something done for a change."

"I need to think about it."

"Fuck that. The meeting with Loggins is tomorrow. I want to head that off."

"You're out of your mind. You want to do this *tonight*?"

"Why not?"

"We'd have to locate him. Check his movements, vehicles, his mates . . ."

"I know where he lives. He works for Max Wilton, the bookie, and I know where he lives too. How hard can it be to find them?"

The park was emptying as the light began to fade and the people and their dogs went home to their dinners. I was feeling let down by my failure to galvanize Ian Gallagher. I hadn't expected this degree of caution and concern for correct procedure. I was beginning to think I'd misjudged my man. Was he thinking about reporting straight to his bosses and instead of putting the pressure on Teacher putting it on me first? I thought I had a strategy for stopping that, but now I wasn't so sure. Gallagher got up suddenly and began to walk around. He went over to the memorial stone and squinted at the faded names. Then he tossed his rolled-up newspaper at a garbage can and scored a direct hit.

Eventually he stopped and put one foot

up on the bench. He rubbed his hand over his face and I could hear the bristles of his beard rasping. "It can't work like that, Hardy. No chance. For one thing, I'm too beat to go cowboying around tonight. For another, whatever you might think, a thing like this needs a bit of groundwork. Where does Teacher live?"

"Coogee."

"Okay. I'll have to have a word with someone out there. Not tell them anything, mind, just get us a bit of elbow room."

That made sense. I'd been keyed up for action and was already feeling the letdown and maybe, just maybe, a little relief. I rolled a cigarette and fiddled with it, not wanting it.

"Look," Gallagher said. "Your information sounds good. Teacher fits the bill perfectly. He's a little guy, and he used to be a gymnast or some fucking thing."

"Boxer," I said.

"Okay. I agree we should shake him up, but not tonight. Tomorrow, after the meeting with Loggins. Let's find out exactly what he has in mind."

"Why?"

"To protect ourselves. What he proposes could be of use to us. Who knows? We might get some sort of open warrant from him, I might. I'll try for it. We'll need all the fucking help we can get. I'm with you. I just don't want to go bull-at-a-gate."

"Like Pascoe."

"Exactly."

"Shit!"

"It's better. Believe me. I can make a few calls tonight. I don't suppose you want to tell me who your mystery informant is? That could help."

I shook my head.

"You don't trust me?"

"I don't trust myself. I haven't told anyone else as much as I've told you. A few people knew little disconnected bits. And I'm keeping away from them, right away."

"That's smart. Let's get what we can out of the meeting with Bob Loggins. Then we can move on Teacher better prepared. I want this to work."

What choices did I have? I wasn't going to go rampaging around the eastern suburbs on my own. My promise to Joan Dare aside, that made no sense. Gallagher evidently had a cool head, something I had always lacked. I argued, but Gallagher had done his thinking and he had the wood on me. It was reasonable to suppose that Teacher and whoever he was working for thought they had contained the matter by killing Meadowbank and Farquhar. They might be on the alert, but they had no reason to suspect any immediate and present danger.

"I've done some work on this," Gallagher said. "Divorces for Redding and Molesworth are in the works."

Maybe that was the clincher, the awareness that he'd been down more of the tracks than me, maybe it was the buzz I was getting from the lower molar, but I agreed to Gallagher's proposal—meet with Loggins, confer, act. We shook hands. He walked under the arch and up Norton Street toward the town hall. I went through the now quiet park, where the tree shadows were long across the grass and paths, and out to my car. I drove to the restaurant where Cyn and I had had our fight, and I ate pasta and drank red wine. The food was good and the wine soothed my anxious spirit and my troublesome tooth.

18

LOGGINS PUT ON A PAIR OF HALF-MOON glasses and looked at me over the top of them. Far from making him look academic, mild, and inoffensive, they increased his menace. Gallagher, wearing a very smart suit, was sitting on Loggins's right. We were in a small room in the College Street police building, grouped around a table with ashtrays, glasses, and a water carafe. I was smoking. Gallagher had a pack of Marlboros and a lighter in front of him, but he hadn't touched them. Loggins had pushed his ashtray away, which was just as well. Three men smoking in that small space would send up a hell of a cloud, and the windows appeared to be sealed. An air conditioner was humming. The room was cool and we all had our jackets on. I'd surrendered my gun at the front desk.

"I've seconded Detective Gallagher onto this team, Hardy," Loggins said. "He's picked up some information relevant to our problem. Ian, over to you."

I tensed. Was Gallagher going to double-cross me? Tell all I knew, claim credit for it somehow, and still dangle me as bait for Chalky Teacher? Gallagher lit a cigarette and began talking. After a few sentences I relaxed. He said he'd heard that a very valuable commodity was at stake in the Meadowbank divorce.

Loggins grinned. "Wait till you hear this."

"A knighthood," Gallagher said.

Loggins got his reaction—I was *very* surprised. "A what?"

"Going rate's fifty grand," Gallagher said. "Cash down. The whisper is that Mrs. Beatrice Meadowbank is lining up to marry a bloke who's paid his money. He won't get the gong though, if he's linked with a woman who's cited in a divorce case. That's why Meadowbank was providing the co-re, so his wife would look pure and innocent."

"And why it was bad news when he looked like he was backing out," Loggins said. "That was a useful contribution from you, Hardy, courtesy of your client."

I was getting confused. Had I passed that on to Gallagher? I wasn't sure. I nodded modestly. "Who's the knight-to-be?"

"I don't know," Gallagher said. "I'm working on it, now that Bob's given me a freer hand."

This was tending in the right direction. I rolled a cigarette and concentrated on getting the ends right. "Still a bit messy, isn't it? For Mrs. M., I mean. Hubby shot down in the street . . ."

"I'm a Catholic," Loggins said. "Marrying a widow's okay, and the innocent party in a divorce case isn't too bad these days. The guilty party's out, but . . . I reckon Mrs. Meadowbank's intended is a Catholic."

Gallagher nodded. "It's a strong possibility, Bob. The thing is, Hardy, this is all very delicate, as you can imagine."

"Political," I said.

Loggins removed his half-glasses. "Right. I want to keep it all tight between the three of us until there's something solid to go on."

I couldn't help letting a skeptical look come over my face. "Inspector, this is the sort of thing that gets tucked away. You know that as well as I do."

"No!" Loggins said fiercely. "I don't know that. This is a criminal matter. Two fucking homicides that I want off the books."

Gallagher stubbed out his cigarette. "Fifty thousand dollars is quite a lot of money. It doesn't just go into one pocket. This can lead in a lot of different directions."

I was putting off asking Loggins the big question. I looked at Gallagher. "Can you tell me where you picked this stuff up?"

"From a man named Vernon Morris. He's a clerk in Alistair Menzies's office. I believe you know him?"

"I've met him, yes."

"He got wind of it, and he owed me a favor."

"Okay," Loggins said. "The question is,

what happens next? That's where you come in, Hardy."

Loggins had arranged to give an interview to a reporter in which my name would be mentioned "off the record." The reporter was notorious for not respecting this convention, and the implication would be that I knew what lay behind the Meadowbank and Farquhar murders. He intended to talk to Andrew Perkins and allow the same impression to be conveyed. Loggins was convinced that Perkins was more deeply involved than it presently appeared.

"Mrs. Meadowbank went to the country straight after the funeral," Gallagher said. "She gets back today. You're going to see her and make a bloody nuisance of yourself. If she knows what's going on, word will travel."

I didn't like the sound of that, and said so.

"Tough luck, Hardy," Loggins snapped. "We've got enough on you to put your pissy little business down the toilet."

"I thought you liked me, Inspector."

"I like the idea of clearing this mess up and sticking it to a few people who deserve it, like Perkins and these idiots who want to be sirs. I like the thought of promotion for Detective Gallagher and myself."

"Good motivation," I said. "Assistant Commissioner Robert Loggins. Sound ring to that."

"Fuckin' oath," Loggins said.

They were doing the rough old cop, smooth young cop, and not with any great finesse. Gallagher cut in with "I can possibly do a bit through the professional channels with Morris. He's decidedly dodgy."

I hated every word of it—the attitudes, the contempt and condescension—and I couldn't help being ballsy. "Detective Gallagher's got a law degree," I said to Loggins. "Did you know that?"

"I don't give a shit," Loggins said. "Are you going to do what you're told, or not?"

"How about my protection?"

Loggins relaxed. This was more his territory—people in fear. "I understand you've got a wife. Any kids?"

"No. And my wife's in Queensland for a bit."

"Good. That makes things easier. This is an eastern-suburbs matter—Perkins, Meadowbank, Farquhar—all on that side. You and Gallagher are inner-west types. That's good too. Gallagher'll look after you 'round the clock. He's Darlinghurst-based, so he's got some idea of the area. I'm a Coogee man myself. You'll be all right, Hardy."

"I grew up in Maroubra," I said. "Maybe we can all go surfing when this is over."

Loggins consulted his watch. "We can't hang on to this room much longer. Have you got any serious problems, Hardy?"

I considered the question seriously. Loggins had come up with a more or less credible plan along the lines he'd outlined previously. Gallagher had supplied a new wrinkle that suggested he knew a useful thing or two and was in touch with the right people. I didn't like the idea of being a worm on a hook, but Gallagher had apparently kept the faith about my information, hadn't he? We had another, more positive agenda. I thought I caught a slight nod from Gallagher. I gave the moment a bit of air, poured some water and drank it slowly, collected up my smoking materials and stowed them away in my pockets. I pushed my chair back.

"I'll go along with it all, Inspector. As you say, I haven't got much choice. I assume I can get my bloody gun back at the front desk. And that I can claim expenses from the police department if I run the mileage up."

"Well, that was bright," Gallagher said as we left the building. "What did you want to go and antagonize him for?"

"I didn't like his attitude. I notice he didn't issue you a permit to break down any door you liked."

Gallagher laughed. He'd been tense in the meeting, but he was relaxing visibly now. We turned the corner into Liverpool Street. I'd left my Falcon in the Goulburn Street parking lot. I had my gun on my hip, and the meeting had made me edgy and anxious for some action. Gallagher strode along beside me. He was about two inches shorter than me, but he was athletic and fit and had no trouble keeping up. He said he'd walked from the Darlinghurst station, which was a fair trot on a warm morning.

"We should have mentioned the ballistics results," Gallagher said. "No match. Meadowbank and Farquhar were killed with different guns."

I shrugged. We entered the parking lot and climbed the stairs to the level where I was parked. Gallagher's heels rang on the concrete and echoed in the enclosed space. He was moving and acting very confidently, so I assumed he had things to tell me. I unlocked the car.

"We've got a few calls to make," he said. "Be better to use your car than one of ours. Unless you meant that crack about the mileage."

I drove down the ramps, paid the fee, and came out on Castlereagh Street. "Are you going to tell me what's on your mind," I said, "or do I have to guess?"

"You're in a shitty mood, Hardy. It's no way to be. Relax."

I didn't want to play by Loggins's rules, and I didn't know what Gallagher's rules were. Either way, I was taking orders, not controlling things, and I didn't like the feeling. Gallagher's suave, calm manner was beginning to annoy me. I drove into Ultimo and pulled up outside the *Sydney News* building. That shook him.

"Jesus Christ! What're we doing here?"

"I'm thinking of a whole new approach,"

I said. "I know a few people in there. I'm thinking about walking in and giving one of them the whole story, lock, stock, and barrel. It might be a way out for me."

"What d'you mean, the whole story?"

"Everything. Including what went on in that meeting just now and including the way you're having such fun playing it so close to your bloody vest. You can come in if you like, supply a few good quotes."

He loosened his tie, the first sign of uncertainty. I was well ahead of him there—I wasn't wearing a tie. He took out a Marlboro and tapped it on the box. "I'm sorry," he said.

"That's a start. Is all this knighthood business on the up-and-up?"

He lit the cigarette. "It is, and there might be more than one knighthood involved."

"Good stuff for the story."

"Get serious, Hardy. What do you want?"

"I want to know if we're going after Chalky Teacher or not."

"Of course we are."

"When? Now?"

Gallagher looked at his watch. "It's up to you. The bloke I want to see knows where

Teacher is going to eat lunch today. Would you rather go up against him before or after he's eaten?"

"He doesn't drink, so it doesn't matter. Before. Where do we find this bloke?"

"Coogee. Let's get going or Chalky'll be well into his steak and chips."

I started the engine and moved off. Gallagher felt around his seat and I asked him what he was doing.

"No seat belts in this crate?"

"No. There's so much rust in the chassis I doubt they'd hold."

"Shit. Why'd you drive a car like this? The suspension's shot too."

"Going to issue me an unroadworthy notice?"

"Someone should. Seat belts're compulsory now. Haven't you heard—'Buckle Up and Live'? Interesting game, advertising. I nearly went into it myself."

I turned out of Cleveland Street into Anzac Parade and moved to the center lane, ready to go left at Alison Road. Gallagher squashed his butt out in the flimsy ashtray and brushed carefully at his neat suit. I couldn't judge his mood—it varied somewhere between relaxed and excited. He lit another cigarette, the first time I'd seen him smoke two that close together. He offered me the pack and I refused.

"You like those rollies?"

"Helps me keep it down. I can't smoke when I'm driving in the city. And it gives me something to do with my hands. You can take five minutes to roll a smoke if you want to. Why did you join the force, Ian? More money in law . . . or advertising."

"There's more to life than money."

"True." I swung left into Alison Road. We went past the Thoroughbred Motel, where Cyn and I had spent a memorable night in our courtship after I'd returned from an interstate trip. Cyn was still a student then. Suddenly I missed her and wanted to tap into the well of experience and feeling and talk we'd built up over the years. Gallagher and I rolled on eastward. Just past the racecourse he stabbed a finger at the sidewalk.

"Stop here. I have to make a call."

He got out and used a phone booth on the sidewalk. I watched as he felt in his pockets, dropped his money in, and dialed—the perfect public servant. I was uneasy though.

He was slipping back into his secretive mode. Who was he calling, and why? Would he tell me? I'd have liked to make a call or two myself—to Vernon Morris maybe, or to Virginia Shaw, or Joan Dare. But then Gallagher was back in the car, all toothy grins and confidence.

"Hoadley Street, Coogee," he said. "Number ten. Just for a second—then we'll know where we're really going."

I started the car and revved it more than I needed to. The irritation was back. "Your informant is what—male or female? Animal, vegetable, or mineral?"

Gallagher didn't reply, which was probably to his credit. I drove on toward Coogee, feeling the pangs of hunger, stabs of pain from my disturbed tooth, and deeper concerns. I tried to tell myself that two big tough men would be more than a match for one little tough man. But I couldn't quite believe it.

19

THE PLACE GALLAGHER DIRECTED ME TO resembled a fortress. It was at the end of a dead-end street and occupied three sizable blocks. There was a tennis court at the back. Substantial wire fences seemed to run around the whole perimeter apart from the front, where big metal gates were set in a brick wall six feet high. The house was a cream-color brick, two-story job with white columns and bay windows. Cyn would have had it dynamited. There was a three-car garage at the end of a wide concrete drive that shone white under the morning sun. Gallagher got out, spoke into an intercom attached to the gates, and waved me inside as they swung open.

There was going to be oil from my leaking gearbox and rubber from my battered tires on the driveway, but I supposed they had some way of dealing with that. I got out of the car and joined Gallagher on the path that led to the front door. The path was a series of round sandstone slices set in a glossy lawn.

"Your snitches live well," I said.

"He's not my snitch."

The door opened before we reached it, and a small man in faded jeans, sneakers, and a black T-shirt nodded to Gallagher.

We walked through the house, not an interesting walk but a long one. It was all deep carpet and chandeliers and attempts at good taste that missed by a mile. We went out through glass doors to a patio overlooking the tennis court and swimming pool. Not such a good view of the sea, but you can't have everything. Two men were sitting at a table under a sun umbrella. Both wore business shirts and ties. One had a pistol in a shoulder holster. The unarmed man, a chunky type with a dark tan and curling gray hair, stood up as he saw Gallagher. His eyes swept over me appraisingly, no doubt arriving at the conclusion that I didn't have a tennis court or a swimming pool.

"This him, Ian?" he said. His voice was deep, with a trace of Irish in it. He was a well-used thirty or a well-preserved fifty, it was hard to tell.

"Yes," Gallagher said.

That was when the small guy in the jeans gripped me in a hold that I'd been taught in the army but never perfected. It paralyzed both my arms between shoulder and elbow. I got set to kick someone or something, but Gallagher had got his gun out, moved around, and pointed it at my right knee.

"Just keep still, Cliff," he said. "He's got a thirty-eight on his left hip, Chalky. Better get it."

By then I was too amazed to do anything. I felt the grip relax, but still couldn't move my arms. Then the weight of the gun left me and I was tasting something bitter in my mouth.

"Nice gun," Teacher said. His voice was gravelly, and I'd heard it before—in St. Peters Lane. He spun the chamber and cocked the revolver. Then he put the muzzle at the point of my jaw, not far from my bad tooth.

"Let's keep it sophisticated," the man in charge said. "My name is Henry Wilton, Hardy. I'm sure you've heard of me."

Of course I had. Wilson and Wilton and Associates was a medium-size private-investigation firm, based in Sydney but with at least one interstate branch. The name Wilton, as Teacher's employer, had almost rung a bell with Joan Dare and should have rung one with me, connecting up with the talk of there being other private detectives involved in the Meadowbank *et al.* divorces. Too late now. Wilton could see how my mind was working. He chuckled and sat back down. "Chalky works for my father, Max. He likes horses. He also works for me because he likes money and other things."

I was left standing there, waiting for sensation to return to the pinched nerves of my upper arms and feeling like an idiot. Teacher was somewhere behind me with a gun; Gallagher was in front of me, also armed, like the dark-haired man still sitting at the table, not paying us a lot of attention. Wilton and I were the only ones without weapons, which put us on a level, in a way. I stepped to my left and went forward, brushing past Gallagher, until I could get my backside lowered onto the low wall of the patio. I took out the makings and rolled a cigarette with cramped but steady fingers. I lit it and looked at Wilton. "You're a shameful disgrace to our profession, Wilton," I said. "I think Wilson should have a word with you."

Give him his due, he laughed. "There isn't any Wilson. Hasn't been for a long time. As for the profession, it's not a bad game, if you know how to go about it the right way, which you clearly don't."

I blew some smoke and moved my shoulders slightly. Felt all right. "Tell me," I said.

Gallagher put his pistol away and took off his jacket, trying to join the administrative rather than the executive branch. "I don't think there's any need to tell him things, Henry," he said. "I think this is his first fucking case."

But Henry Wilton's weakness was showing; he liked to talk, especially about himself, and maybe he didn't get too many safe opportunities to do that. He settled back into the shade of the umbrella. "I can't see the harm,

Ian, old son," he said. "Seeing that it's possibly his last fucking case."

The effort never had much chance, but I made it anyway. I flicked the cigarette butt at Gallagher and scored a hit somewhere on his face. I launched myself from the wall and made a clawing grab at the gun sitting in the armpit of the dark man who was yet to say a word. My reactions were way too slow, and my target was much too fast. He clamped his arm over the gun and hit me with a short elbow jolt. Then Teacher stepped in and thumped me in the ribs. I stumbled and sagged back against the wall. Wilton hadn't moved. The only satisfaction I got was Ian Gallagher rubbing at his eyes and swearing when he saw how the cigarette ash had dirtied his shirt.

"Game enough," Wilton said. "It's a pity you're not smart. You had a warning."

"I don't like warnings, or being shot at." I looked at Gallagher, still brushing at his shirt. "Or being bullshitted."

"I have to admit you've had your share. There's still a chance for you, Hardy. I hope you realize that."

I recognized the line for what it was—a

piece of hope with a barbed hook inside—and I didn't respond.

"We'd like to know who put you on to Chalky," Wilton said. "Tell us that, and maybe we can work something out."

"What's the point?" Gallagher said. "It's contained. Let's get it over with."

"Don't be so hasty, Ian. Chalky'd like to know, wouldn't you?"

"That's right," Teacher growled. "But there's no need to ask him nicely."

"There'll be none of that here," Wilton snapped. "How about it, Hardy? Want to chat?"

"I might," I said. "But I'd need to get something in return. I'm having trouble believing this is about divorces and knighthoods."

"I feel like a drink," Wilton said, "especially if we're going to be talking." He nudged the man who'd put his elbow into my face. "Slip inside, Mario, and get out a few bottles and glasses."

Mario moved to obey.

"Henry," Gallagher said, "stop pissing around."

Wilton said, "Contained, wasn't that your

word? No one's expecting him or you, are they?"

"No."

"Relax, then. Have a drink. You've done a good job. You deserve it."

I understand that many people have had this same experience: I have dreamed that I am about to be executed. This was something like those dreams—slow-moving, terrifying, but with a kind of civilized veneer and a feeling that the moment would be long-delayed and maybe never reached. Teacher kept a very close eye on me, and my .38 rested very comfortably in his capable right hand. His boxing career didn't seem to have done him any harm. He might have moved up a weight division, but he still looked very fit. His eyes were steady, like the rest of him—neat, economical movements, no tics. No bravado either. Wilton was clearly the boss, but I had a sense that Teacher would go free-lance if it suited him.

Mario arrived with several chilled bottles of Resch's pilsner, a collection of frosted glasses, and one paper cup on a tray, which he put down on the table. A tall tree growing near the patio was casting some welcome shade by this time. I was sweating. I didn't sweat in my execution dream as far as I could remember. This was fear. Gallagher looked anxious. Wilton was relaxed until he took stock of the drinks. "What're you doing, Mario?" he said. "Go and get a bitter lemon for Chalky. Right, Chalky?"

Teacher nodded. A man of action, Chalky, like Mario. Neither of them entirely happy with things, like Gallagher, but I couldn't see myself recruiting them as allies. The only happy member of the party, now that he was about to get a drink in his hand and everyone was doing his bidding, was Henry Wilton. Mario poured the drinks. I accepted my paper cup and sipped cautiously. It would have been easy for Mario to have slipped something into the cup, and icy cold beer will conceal most tastes. But why should they bother? I never heard of truth serum in tablet form, and if they wanted to subdue me they had Chalky, willing and able.

Wilton drained his glass and signaled for Mario to refill it. Gallagher smoked moodily and drank slowly. Teacher took his soft drink straight from the bottle. A tough guy's tough guy. Mario poured half a glass for himself, took a sip, and lost interest. It was hard to guess what Mario would really be interested in —maybe a Gucci shotgun.

"Well, now," Wilton said. "Ian here says he thinks you're pretty smart, Hardy. Are you smart enough to talk yourself out of trouble?"

"I don't feel very smart just now," I said. "But you're a good talker and I'm a good listener."

Wilton worked on his second beer for a while. He traced patterns on the tabletop with the moisture from his glass and appeared to be trying to make a decision. Eventually he erased the doodling. "Okay. You might even be useful. The knighthoods *are* important. These silvertails want them more than they want to fuck, and if the state and federal governments change, that'll be the end of the game around here. The price has never been higher, and there's a lot of characters getting in for their chop. Redding's not the only politician, and there's a judge who'd eat his wig to be a sir."

"I can't see that a few divorces would matter much," I said. I shot a look at Gallagher, who was half-turned away, staring toward the visible sliver of ocean. "But I suppose there's time and money involved, and when someone pulls out, like Meadowbank did . . ."

"That's right. And the blokes panting for the nod get impatient. And Bob Askin and his mates can up the ante. Sorry, didn't mean to mention any names."

"Shit, Henry," Gallagher said.

Wilton wiped foam from his mouth. "Shut your face. We want something from this man."

"You won't get it," Gallagher said.

"We'll see."

Mario yawned, and Wilton gave him a dirty look. "You know what discretion statements are, don't you, Hardy?"

I did, courtesy of my one, less than wholly successful year of law studies—statements lodged with the court by divorce petitioners, suing on the grounds of their partners's transgressions, giving details of their own misdoings. It was a requirement of the crazy, outdated divorce law, particularly if the "innocent" party was seeking custody of children. Mostly, these statements went unread by anyone, but sometimes a judge who smelled a rat or disliked one of the parties would take a discretion statement into consideration. "I know about them," I said.

Wilton lifted his glass in a sort of toast. "How many women have you fucked since you were married?"

I didn't answer.

"Be quite a few in my case, and some names I wouldn't want known. Do you get my drift?"

"Blackmail. You've got hold of some discretion statements—"

"A stack of 'em."

"That sounds like *real* money."

"Believe me, it is."

"And some people got greedy, like Juliet Farquhar?"

Wilton shook his head. "Silly girl. She was very cooperative and very useful for a time, working from Andrew Perkins's office. She helped with the documentation, you might say."

"She sicced Chalky on me too."

"She didn't know what she was doing," Wilton said. "When she put a few things together she wasn't so cooperative and . . ." He spread his hands. He wore a broad gold wedding ring. His hands were well cared for and very clean.

I held out my paper cup in Mario's direction, but he ignored me. "Who performed that little service?"

I caught a twitch from Mario.

"Which brings us to Virginia Shaw," I said.

"That bitch! She just threw you in it, mate. She knew the score. Whose name's in half those discretion statements, d'you reckon?"

"What was the problem?"

"Gave her a grip, didn't it? Now you're *really* talking greedy. We'd like you to help us with her whereabouts."

I shook my head.

Gallagher slammed his empty glass down on the table. "That's enough, Henry! I helped you set up this fucking thing, steered you through it. Now I'm saying that's enough running off at the mouth to this joker. Ask him the question."

Henry Wilton wasn't a stupid man. He knew when he'd had his own way long enough and how to give ground graciously. "I think you're right, Ian. Our cards are on the table, Hardy. Who gave you Chalky's name?"

No one was pretending to be polite anymore, and negotiation wasn't in the air. Wilton had enjoyed telling his story, but it hadn't given me any room to maneuver. Perhaps more had come out than he'd intended. The upshot was that I was transformed from a captive audience into something disposable, and we both knew it.

I took out the makings and rolled a cigarette. "I think it was Bob Askin," I said, "but it might have been Tiny Tim."

Chalky Teacher hit me high and low, very hard. I didn't see either of the punches coming, and after they landed I didn't see or hear anything at all.

20

PAIN AND FEAR ARE GOOD COMPANIONS.
They go together well. Back each other up
like a good doubles pair at tennis. I had both
of them with me when I regained conscious-
ness after Chalky Teacher's scientific assault.
The pain was in my head, hands, and feet, and
just about everywhere else in between. I tried
to move to ease it and found out the main
cause: I was tied at the wrists and ankles, with
my hands behind my back and my legs drawn
up. Spasms of cramp shot through me as I

tried to move. I lay still, waiting for the agony to settle back into ordinary pain. The fear was internal and external. I was sweating; there was a foul taste in my mouth, which was taped shut; and my bowels were agitating fitfully like an off-balance washing machine.

I opened my eyes and experienced a surge of panic. I couldn't see anything. Had Chalky blinded me? Then I realized I was in an enclosed, lightless space. Or almost lightless. I blinked and let my eyes adapt. Amid the blackness were patches of gray, some paler than others. I felt rather than saw the confinement, but I knew it was very close. A big box? A cupboard? I tried not to think of a coffin—it was bigger than that. Then an engine started and the prison began to move. I felt the wheels under me bumping along. I was in the back of some kind of vehicle, a small truck, a van, or a station wagon. The windows were blacked out, and the doors or hatch were a tight fit.

Trussed up like that, I felt like a thing, a nonperson, an object being transported to some unknown destination. After a while I could move slightly without bringing on the cramp, but there was no point to it. I couldn't move enough to gauge the dimensions of the space, and what the hell difference did it make anyway? I was tied so tightly I couldn't get leverage of any kind. There was no possibility of rolling over or sitting up without dislocating several joints. Suddenly, I was aware of another sensation—cold. I was naked apart from my jockettes, and small draughts were blowing over me and making me shiver.

At first I couldn't understand that. It was a warm day, wasn't it? Then I realized I had no idea of the time. Warm days change to cool nights. How long had I been unconscious? In a way, that lost time and not knowing its duration were the most frightening things of all. They gave me the feeling that I was already dead. I closed my eyes again and concentrated on trying to get some movement in the lashings around my ankles and wrists. Nothing, not a fraction of an inch. I probed with my tongue against the tape across my mouth, but it was wide, heavy-duty stuff, generously applied. I panicked again, almost choked, and forced myself to breathe regularly through my nose. I was pretty sure I was experiencing the hard way another one of Chalky Teacher's great talents.

I eventually decided I was in a panel van. The engine noise was muffled, meaning that there was a solid barrier between me and the front of the vehicle. Not a station wagon therefore, and some branches brushing the roof overhead gave me an idea of its height. Too low for a truck. I settled on a panel van—a matter of the quality of the ride and the pitch of the rattles and squeaks. I tried to listen to the traffic outside to get an idea of time and place, but wheels on roads sound much the same. The vehicle stopped and started, turned left and right, rode rough and smooth. I heard the occasional rumble and air brakes of a truck, like on a tourist bus. I heard no train noises or jet engines. I didn't have a clue where I was.

Then I did, in a very general way. The road got rougher and narrower, judging from the way the left-side wheels dipped off the asphalt from time to time, and the traffic was definitely lighter. The country. I'm a city man who prefers pavement to paddocks, and I never preferred it more strongly than at that moment. It's too easy to lose things and citizens in the country. There's too much space and not enough people to notice. Another opinion is that everybody knows everybody else out there and nothing goes undiscussed. A nice debating point, but I couldn't see that it was going to make much difference to me one way or the other.

All this mental activity diverted me from my aches and pains, if not from my terrors. I doubted that they'd torture me to extract the name of the person who'd tipped me off about Teacher or to get a line on Virginia Shaw. It takes a special kind of nastiness to do that. I'd seen it in Malaya in Australians, Brits, Malays, and Chinese—I didn't see it in Teacher or Gallagher. Mario was a possible candidate. It was more likely that they were just tidying up, and that was quite frightening enough. I tried to think of something I might bargain with, some threat to worry them. There was nothing. Fear of dying is ignominious. Life itself becomes precious, whatever its quality. I just wanted the impossible—for the painful, cold, humiliating ride to go on and on.

A jolting stop, and I knew it was the final one. Doors opening and closing. Voices, and then the sound of something being taken down from a roof rack. A rustling noise and then the clank of metal. It wasn't a surfboard.

The opening of the back of my box confirmed my guess about the sort of vehicle I'd been traveling in. A strong flashlight beam lit up the interior, danced around, and hit me, blindingly, in the face. I shut my eyes against it, and it moved away. I blinked and looked past it, out at the dark shapes of trees outlined against a starlit night sky.

"I think it's going to rain," a voice I didn't recognize said. *Mario?*

"Good. Make the fuckin' ground softer." That was Teacher.

A match flared and I smelled tobacco smoke. "Let's just get on with it, eh?" Ian Gallagher was nervous. Maybe it was his first time at a cold-blooded execution and interment. If so, I had to hope he wasn't the one to do the job. A pistol shot at close range can go terribly wrong. I was feeling calm now—registering every little thing as if my system was working frantically for the short time it had left to function—but resigned. My feet were grabbed and I was pulled out of the van without any regard for my well-being. I lost skin, suffered wrenched joints, and my head banged painfully as it crossed the gap between the van floor and the flap of the bottom half of the door. A final heave and I collapsed onto cool, damp, sweet-smelling grass.

I fell on my face and struggled to roll over. It hurt everywhere, but I managed it. I looked up into the pale, troubled eyes of Ian Gallagher. One part of my brain was telling me that it was better they should leave the tape across my mouth. Meant they weren't going to get out the bolt cutters. I was worried about that clank from the roof rack. But I didn't want to die like a dumb animal, I *wanted* to speak. Gallagher drew on his cigarette and looked away.

"Here?" Mario said. He glanced at the sky. It had been him worrying about the rain. I would have welcomed a few drops. I was hungry for sensation, experience, touch, sound, and feel as my time ran out. I wanted to stretch the moments, suck just a little more of the juice of life, even though it had turned sour and scary.

"Why not here?" Teacher said.

The next sound I heard was a familiar one—my .38 cocks smoothly and softly if you know how to handle a weapon. Teacher did. I kept my eyes open, even though the blood pounding in my head threatened to burst through my eyeballs. I wanted to see things, hear things! Mario was holding the flashlight, and in its glancing beam I saw what he held in his other fist—a short-handled shovel. That's when I closed my eyes and said my good-byes to Cyn and my sister and Joanie Dare and everybody else I'd loved and hurt.

When the heavy, booming shots sounded I knew the bullets weren't for me, and I experienced sheer joy. Teacher was hit twice. He jerked the gun up and fired wildly, but another shot got him somewhere vital and he crumpled and lay still. Mario was hit too. He yelled, dropped the shovel and the flashlight, and started to run toward the trees. Two more bullets stopped him in his tracks. He groaned, fell awkwardly, and twitched. I heard him scratching at the ground. The flashlight was on its side, still throwing light. I twisted my head around to see Gallagher. As I did a voice came from the darkness:

"One fuckin' move, Ian, and you're off."

Another light showed, and Colin Pascoe came slowly forward carrying a carbine and a large flashlight. The beam reached Gallagher, who stood white-faced and shaking. His jacket was buttoned. He hadn't tried to reach for his pistol.

"I knew you were a gutless wonder," Pascoe said. He walked up to Gallagher and clouted him hard in the face with the metal flashlight. Gallagher reeled back and hit the open door of the van. He grabbed at it for support. Blood trickled down his face. "Col, I—"

"Shut up, prick! Put your weapon on the ground."

Gallagher eased the pistol out slowly and dropped it onto the grass. It landed only a foot or so from my head, and the sound reawakened my fears. Three enemies out of action, but what about Pascoe? I squinted up at him, but the light wasn't on him and all I could see was a big dark shape. Then I was blinded by the strong beam and I heard Pascoe's rumbling laugh. "I wondered why your big mouth wasn't working, Hardy. Now I see."

The light danced away again. Pascoe picked up Gallagher's gun and shoved it into a pocket of his combat jacket. He had to juggle the other things he was holding, but he did it deftly. This was the moment for him to swing the carbine around and make it a hat trick, if that was what he had in mind. Gallagher was fumbling for a cigarette.

"Light me one too, Ian," Pascoe said. "You should be able to manage that."

Pascoe put his flashlight on my chest. Gallagher passed the lit cigarette over. They were virtually on top of me, and Pascoe's rifle was only inches from my head. He drew on his cigarette and blew out a cloud of smoke, then he leaned the rifle against the van. It was very quiet. Mario's dirt-scratching had stopped. Gallagher and Pascoe smoked. I shivered and the light jiggled.

"Chalky's where he belongs at last," Pascoe said. "Who's the other cunt?"

Gallagher's voice was strangled and shaky. "Name's Mario. He works for—"

"Henry Wilton. I was watching. You might have a fuckin' law degree, but you're a dumb bastard, Ian. I knew you were bent. I've been watching you ever since you got into this. I heard your little chat with Hardy in his office."

Jack the rat, I thought, *and he isn't going to kill me.*

"What . . . what're you going to do, Col?"

"Do? I've already done what Bob Loggins asked me to do."

"Loggins. What d'you mean?"

"Oh, me 'n Bob go back a long way. He told me what was going on and I agreed to keep an eye on you and Hardy. It worked out pretty much the way he hoped it would, eh?"

I was seriously cold now, trembling, and my various cuts and bruises were stinging and stiffening up. I made an effort, heaved, and flipped the flashlight off my chest.

"Shit, I forgot about you, Hardy. Cut him loose, Ian, and see if you can find something to keep the poor bugger warm."

I knew enough to lie still for a minute after Gallagher cut the rope. A sudden movement could've given me a crippling cramp. He ripped the tape from my face roughly, taking skin and beard bristles with it. I swore at him as I slowly tested the mobility of my arms and legs. He made no reply. He went to the van and came back with my clothes, which he dropped on top of me. I turned slowly and painfully to look at Pascoe, who was squashing out the end of his cigarette with his big, blunt fingers. He dropped the butt into his pocket.

"Thanks," I said. My voice sounded like a frog with its throat cut. "Where are we?"

"Out Campbelltown way," Pascoe said. "You were bloody lucky, Hardy. It was tricky following them in the dark with no lights, and if they'd got on with the job instead of pissing around, you'd be under by now."

I pulled the crumpled clothes on, making small, careful movements, glad of the warmth, even gladder to get the feeling that I was still the same man, still alive, and likely to see the night out. "You sound almost sorry they didn't do it."

Pascoe laughed, picked up Mario's flashlight, and walked across to look at the dead men. He barely glanced at the neat, dark shape that was Teacher, but he studied the crumpled form of Mario closely, playing the light beam on different parts of the body. He straightened up and ambled back. "I got him twice with the carbine, but he got another nick as well."

"From Chalky," I said. "With my gun."

I stood up. My joints creaked. I'd almost dislocated my shoulder when I'd fallen out of the van, and it was aching savagely. Ian Gallagher was chain-smoking, staring out toward the stand of trees. His pale face was set in lines of despair, and his usually carefully arranged fair hair had flopped down over his forehead, giving him a defeated, puzzled look. My keys, watch, and tobacco were in the side pockets of my jacket. My pistol holster was missing. I looked at my watch. It was close to 10:00 P.M. I rolled a cigarette, one of the worst I'd ever made, and got it up to my mouth. My lighter, Cyn's present, was missing, and I never found it. Gallagher lit the smoke.

"What happens next?" I asked Pascoe.

21

I GAVE PASCOE A BRIEF RUNDOWN ON
what the whole business had been all about
and ventured the opinion that Mario had
killed Juliet Farquhar. Gallagher nodded, but
stopped the movement when Pascoe gave him
a savage look. The rain held off, but it was
getting colder out there. Gallagher and I were
in our street clothes; Pascoe was comfortable
in his battle jacket. He asked the right questions, and I realized that my original assessment of him had been way off-base. He was a

shrewd, experienced cop, and I was having trouble matching him up with the blustering thug who'd assaulted me in the Bondi police station. I asked him about that and he grinned.

"An act," he said. "More or less. I knew Ian here was playing funny buggers. Someone I had keeping an eye out told me about your little powwow outside the Darlinghurst station. When I heard you'd gone straight for Ian after you struck bother I thought I'd push that along a little. You're a pretty good fighter, Hardy, but I wasn't really trying."

I buttoned my jacket against the cold and said nothing. It was still good to be alive but not so good to feel stupid. I was in pain, too, and wanted to get away from the spot that easily could have been my unmarked grave. Pascoe was starting to look a bit tired himself, and Gallagher had become very quiet and still. He wasn't smoking now, just worrying. My tooth jumped.

"You wouldn't have anything alcoholic on you, would you?" I asked Pascoe. "I could do with a drink."

"There's some scotch in the van," Gallagher said.

Pascoe took Gallagher's pistol from his

pocket. "You fetch it, Ian. I'll come along just to make sure you don't drop it in the dark."

I was shivering again by this time. I leaned against the vehicle and my foot touched something stiff but yielding. It was a sheet of heavy plastic. Another shovel and a rake were half-wrapped in it. Standing in the pool of light it was hard to tell much about the plot of land. I thought I could see the track we had come in on; the trees were plain against the sky and there looked to be other shapes— bushes or rocky outcrops. The grass was high and thick. Nothing much had happened out here for a very long time. Then I caught a movement out in the darkness. I stared, and two shining disks appeared a few feet above the ground about fifty yards away. I was laughing when Gallagher and Pascoe came back with the bottle.

"What's funny?" Pascoe said.

I pointed. "There's a kangaroo out there."

Pascoe swung his light. The shining eyes disappeared, and I heard the soft thumps as the animal hopped away.

"Got better things to do," Pascoe said. "So have we."

We all had a drink from the bottle. The liquor stung my battered mouth and scorched my parched throat, but it still felt good.

"Good grog," Pascoe said. "You didn't keep any little mementos, did you? Tapes? Notes? Photos of this and that?"

I shook my head and reached for the bottle again.

"Okay. Well, what we've got here is two fucking murderers killed by a police officer in the course of his duty. We've got another officer operating in an undercover capacity as a witness, and a civilian who'd been assisting authorities in their investigation. Also a witness. What would you say about that assessment of the situation, Mr. Hardy?"

Two big swigs on a very empty stomach and a very disturbed metabolism hit me like a right and a left from Tony Mundine. I was feeling light-headed and weightless, as if I could float away into the trees. Some birds called. Another sip and I could be up there in the trees with them. "I'd say that was spot on, Mr. Pascoe. Spot on."

"Good. Don't touch anything here. Just get in the van to keep warm. Me and Ian'll get some help. We'll be back soon."

Gallagher's face was a study of confusion, a blend of terror and hope. He didn't fancy walking off into the dark with Pascoe, but the reference to him as a witness and an undercover operator must have sounded like sweet music. He took another drink and screwed the cap back on the bottle. No more drinking. No flying tonight.

"What about Ian? Does he get a say?"

"No," Pascoe said. "He does exactly what he's told. He doesn't get a say at all."

That night I discovered how much better the cops are at managing their own death scenes than anyone else's. The blue lights and the uniforms arrived along with the suits and the cameras. They went about it smoothly, with lots of nods and murmurs of agreement. Bob Loggins showed up briefly. He didn't talk to me, but I saw him shake a very pale and stressed-looking Ian Gallagher by the hand. My .38 went into a plastic bag and I never saw it again. A bloke with a medical chest came over to me and did what he could for my cuts and abrasions. He gave me a sling for my wrenched shoulder, and I wore it. Why not? Why should Colin Pascoe hog all the heroism?

Eventually they had all the pictures and measurements and fingerprints they needed, and as the movie people say, they called it a wrap. I was just about asleep by this time, with a blanket around my shoulders. I'd had some hot coffee from a Thermos, but the caffeine was losing the battle. I climbed into the back of a police car and settled down into its comfort. Just before we left, the door opened and I was looking into Pascoe's ugly, bristled face, smelling the whiskey and tobacco on his breath and knowing my breath would smell much the same.

"I'll drop in tomorrow," he said quietly. "Until then your door and your mouth are shut. You don't use the phone, you don't write anything down. Understood?"

"What about Henry Wilton?"

He put his fingers to his lips and slammed the door shut. I don't remember anything about the ride back to Glebe. I must have slept through it. A cop escorted me to my front door and helped me to open it. The cord they'd used on my wrists had scraped skin away, and I realized that my fingers had been tingling unpleasantly ever since the circulation had been restored.

"Will you be all right, Mr. Hardy?"

"I'll be okay, Constable. Thank you."

"Goodnight."

I stood at the door and watched him go down the path and through the gate to the police car. A solidly built young man, competent, a public servant. It was 2:00 A.M. or thereabouts, and the street was quiet. The strangeness of it all struck me—here I was in my scarcely renovated terrace in Glebe, with money being made and upward mobility all around me, and I'd come within a hair's breadth of being buried in a Campbelltown paddock. I was bleeding in ten places and smelled like a wrestler after a night on the town. I didn't belong here, but then again, with an architect wife and a small business to operate, I did. I closed the door and limped toward the back of the quiet house.

A jacket of Cyn's was hanging on a doorknob, and I sniffed at it as I went past. Ma Griffe or Rive Gauche, I could never tell the difference. But it was a Cyn smell, and I missed her powerfully. What would I tell her if she'd been here? Would I say "I came this close?" I knew I wouldn't. I'd make a joke about the steepness of the McElhone steps and the exorbitant cost of dry cleaning and throw down as much white wine as I could. I climbed the stairs, stripping off my clothes as I went, and I fell on the bed and dragged a sheet across me. An hour later I woke from a nightmare, which faded immediately. I was cold, and the room seemed unnaturally dark. I found a blanket and turned on a bedside light and slept fitfully for another couple of hours, like a frightened kid.

As it happened, Pascoe's rules weren't hard to live by. I wasn't in any shape to go out walking, there was food and drink in the house, and I was too demoralized to want to talk to anybody. The phone rang a couple of times and I ignored it. I didn't stick to the letter of the law—I opened the front door to collect the paper. A car I'd never seen before was parked across the street, and it was still there later when I checked for the mail. I read the paper from cover to cover. They were talking about introducing late-night shopping on Thursdays on a trial basis. There was a story about the opening of Sydney's first sex shop, selling "fantasy apparel, erotic literature, and marital aids." Probably go well on Thursday nights. The operational phase of Australia's military presence in Vietnam was drawing to a close. I read a piece about that several times to see what it meant about the war, apart from the fact that the boys were coming home. Between the armyese and the journalese it was impossible to tell.

The mail consisted of several bills and a postcard from Cyn. The picture was a collage of the attractions of Cairns, which seemed to consist of nightclubbing, fishing, waterskiing, and playing golf. There didn't seem to be anything I'd want to do. Cyn had written a few lines in her impeccable private-schoolgirl script to the effect that the weather was great and the job was interesting and Queenslanders were funny folk who called bags "ports" and said "eh?" at the end of every sentence. She missed me, she said. She ended with "Why don't you pack a port and come up, eh?"

I turned the television on and off, listened to a few news broadcasts on the radio, and tried to read Manning Clark's *Short History of Australia* to make up for one of my many educational deficiencies. I liked the book, but my mind kept wandering to the business I'd been through and wasn't finished with yet. It was embarrassing to have misread Pascoe and Gallagher so completely and to have been jerked around like a puppet. I resolved to be a lot more cautious—downright mistrustful—if I stayed in the private-eye game. That was a big question I shied away from. I showered, but my face was too badly roughed-up to shave. I put first-aid cream on my lacerations and probed at my bad tooth with my tongue. It felt loose. Another one on its way out. The shoulder felt better though, and I did without the sling.

Pascoe arrived late in the afternoon. He plunked himself down on the sofa. "Got any beer?"

I opened some Coopers' ale I'd bought for a South Australian friend of Cyn's who turned out not to drink beer. Pascoe took a big, appreciative gulp. I sat in a saucer chair and rolled a cigarette. Pascoe pulled out his Craven A cigarettes. Man-talk time.

"Did you do as I told you, Hardy?"

"You know I did. You had one of your

blokes outside all day. And I bet a couple of the phone calls I didn't take were from you."

He grunted and drank some more beer. "Well, it was a shitty mess you got yourself into. Some big names and some big money there."

"I'm sure you can handle it. What's going to happen to Gallagher?"

"Nothing. As I said, he was working undercover."

"Bullshit. He was right there in the middle of it."

"That's not the way we want it to be. The force can't afford all that to come out just now. But we'll keep an eye on him."

"Wilton'll turn him in."

Pascoe drank some more beer and shook his head.

"Jesus Christ," I said. "This was a bloody big conspiracy. Lawyers, politicians, a cop, God knows who else. And you're just going to leave it at two dead hoods?"

"There's no evidence against Wilton."

"I was *there*."

"So was Ian Gallagher. Forget it, Hardy. Like you say, it's big. Too big for you. It's being handled . . . institutionally, like."

I looked at him—big, solid, not at all stupid as I'd thought, and doing what he thought was best. I wished I had some similar conviction. The phone rang. Pascoe held up his hand to stop me from moving and reached for it himself.

"Yeah? This is Pascoe. We're having a drink and a talk right now."

He cradled the phone under his ear and picked up his glass. Somehow, he was able to drink from it with his head in that position. He looked at me as if I were asking him a big favor. "What?" he said. "Oh, I reckon he'll be all right. Yeah, I'm sure he will be. Thanks."

He hung up and held out his glass for more beer. I poured. The room was smoky now, smelling of hops and still warm from the heat of the day, but it was beginning to take on some of the atmospherics of the Campbelltown paddock. Pascoe looked critically at his beer—there was too big a head.

"I get it," I said. "I play ball and I'm safe."

Pascoe drank. "That's right. Don't worry about it, Hardy. It's all just part of the very difficult business of law enforcement. All you have to do is nothing."

That was more than tempting, it was compelling. There were loose threads though, and pride demanded that I pull a few of them. "Gallagher told me that a man named Vernon Morris in Alistair Menzies's office had put him on to the divorce deal. Anything to that?"

"No. He was lying. You should've checked up on that, Hardy. Could have saved you some grief. Mind you, we mightn't have got this result if you had."

"That's all that matters."

"I'll give you something for free. It was Dick Maxwell put you onto Chalky, right?"

I swallowed the rest of the beer in my glass. "Shit. Don't tell me you had a tail on me when I went to see Maxwell. I'll give this game away—"

"No. We've been doing some sniffing around. Chalky was a bit gay, it seems. Him and Maxwell were friends and then they weren't."

Another thread pulled. Pascoe took out another cigarette, but put it away. He had only an inch of beer left and was obviously getting ready to go. "Well, have you got the picture?"

I nodded and he lifted himself up from the sofa. "Thanks for the drink. I wouldn't say you're actually in credit with us, Hardy. But if you stay sensible you'll be all right, and I might be able to do you some good one of these days. Who knows?"

"I've got a client. Virginia Shaw. What about her?"

"Where is she?"

"Not in Sydney."

Pascoe laughed. He picked up his glass and emptied it. "I think you should tell her to stay where she is and get into another line of work."

"What about the divorces?"

"Watch the papers. There's not going to be any blackmail, I can tell you that. You really look pretty beat, Hardy." He took out his car keys and jiggled them as he looked around the room. I'd left my book and the papers scattered about. My crumpled suit jacket hung on the stair rail, and my dirty shoes were in the hallway. "Where's your wife?"

"In Queensland."

"I reckon you should shoot up there yourself for a holiday."

22

"YOU'VE MADE HALF OF IT UP," GLEN said. "More than half."

"Every word is true. I swear it."

It was into the early hours by the time I'd finished. We were lying together on the sofa, huddled close for the warmth. Even summer nights can get cool in the Hunter. Glen had wrapped herself in an old football sweater that had belonged to her dad. Ted Withers had been a dishonest cop, who'd gotten in very deep and virtually committed suicide to cover up his crookedness. Knowing this, I'd worried about telling the story to Glen. She was protective of the good parts of her father's memory and still a loyal member of the New South Wales police force. But we'd both had a fair bit to drink and it was all a long time ago.

"So what happened?"

"Who to?"

"All of them. Wilton."

"Nothing much. He went quiet for a while, seemed to be strapped for cash."

"You mean he was paying someone off?"

"I don't know. His father died and he took over the bookmaking business. I've seen him in Coogee once or twice."

"Gallagher?"

I poured the last dregs of a bottle into my glass. Glen had switched to tea a few hours back, but I'd gone on killing brain cells. "He resigned a few years later and joined the force in Queensland. Got pretty high up too. I saw his name mentioned in a report on the Fitzgerald hearings. He was in the hot seat over some kind of corruption. I don't know how it all came out."

"What about Pascoe and Loggins? I'm pretty sure I've heard of Loggins."

"You would have. He only retired a few years back. He made Assistant Commissioner. A very distinguished career. Col Pascoe made senior rank. We kept in touch. He was useful to me a few times later. He had a heart attack while he was playing golf at Concord and dropped dead in a bunker. It's one of the reasons I've never played golf. Mind you, he was smoking fifty a day, so it's probably one of the reasons I gave up smoking as well."

"Thank God. A smoking golfer, I don't think I could stand it. There must have been an inquest on the two dead men."

"There was. I don't remember much about it. Staged, you'd call it. I said my piece. Pascoe and Gallagher got commendations. I didn't feel too bad about that—Chalky and Mario were no loss."

"Double standard there, Cliff. You see Henry Wilton in Coogee, and he was the real villain."

I yawned. "Just being realistic. I don't place bets with him."

I hadn't thought about all this in a long time, and now that they were back the memories weren't pleasant. Glen could feel the tension in me and she touched my face. "You healed up okay. Is that the most dangerous situation you've been in?"

"I think it's the closest I've come since Malaya, yes. There've been some tough moments since, but I was completely helpless that time, just waiting, just feeling stupid."

I remembered that it had taken me some time to get my confidence back. I let things slide, lost jobs, didn't do much at all for a few weeks. Then I told myself that I'd gone in at the deep end and it couldn't be that hard all the time. And I *had* done a few things right, like throwing the camera at Teacher, locating Maxwell, and keeping Joanie Dare's name from Gallagher. I was never able to give her the story though, and I couldn't explain why. She accused me of bad faith, and that was the end of our friendship. I worked my way back to normal via some easy jobs, had a few lucky breaks, and eventually put the whole thing behind me. I hung on to the old Falcon, but I got a new gun.

"Which brings us to the next question," Glen said.

"It's late, love. We should go to bed."

"I want to hear about Cyn, and now's the best time. Did you go up to Queensland?"

I shook my head. "I called her with that in mind, but we had a fight over the phone. I don't even remember what it was about. Something stupid. So I didn't go. She came back and we struggled on for a while, but she left in the end."

"Where is she now?"

"On the north shore somewhere. She married an advertising man. They've got a couple of kids, and she sails or skis or something."

"Not friends?"

"Not anything."

Glen moved closer to me and I held her. There was sand in the part of her hair. I touched the long white scar the bullet wound had left in her arm, smoothing out the puckered skin. "Nice," she murmured. "And what would you say you learned from all that?"

"I became a very much better judge of the police," I said.

Match wits with the best-selling
MYSTERY WRITERS
in the business!

SUSAN DUNLAP
"Dunlap's police procedurals have the authenticity of telling detail."
—*The Washington Post Book World*

☐ AS A FAVOR	20999-4	$3.99
☐ ROGUE WAVE	21197-2	$4.99
☐ DEATH AND TAXES	21406-8	$4.99

SARA PARETSKY
"Paretsky's name always makes the top of the list when people talk about the new female operatives." —*The New York Times Book Review*

☐ BLOOD SHOT	20420-8	$5.99
☐ BURN MARKS	20845-9	$5.99
☐ INDEMNITY ONLY	21069-0	$5.99
☐ GUARDIAN ANGEL	21399-1	$5.99
☐ KILLING ORDERS	21528-5	$5.99

SISTER CAROL ANNE O'MARIE
"Move over Miss Marple..." —*San Francisco Sunday Examiner & Chronicle*

☐ ADVENT OF DYING	10052-6	$3.99
☐ THE MISSING MADONNA	20473-9	$3.50
☐ A NOVENA FOR MURDER	16469-9	$3.99
☐ MURDER IN ORDINARY TIME	21353-3	$4.99

ANTHONY BRUNO
"The best fictional cop duo around." —*People*

☐ BAD BUSINESS	21120-4	$4.99
☐ BAD GUYS	21363-0	$4.99
☐ BAD MOON	21559-5	$4.99

LINDA BARNES
☐ COYOTE	21089-5	$4.99
☐ STEEL GUITAR	21268-5	$4.99

At your local bookstore or use this handy page for ordering:

DELL READERS SERVICE, DEPT. DGM
2451 South Wolf Rd., Des Plaines, IL. 60018

Please send me the above title(s). I am enclosing $_____.
(Please add $2.50 per order to cover shipping and handling.) Send check or money order—no cash or C.O.D.s please.

Ms./Mrs./Mr. _____

Address _____

City/State _____ Zip _____

DGM-3/94

Prices and availability subject to change without notice. Please allow four to six weeks for delivery.

Robert B. PARKER

"The toughest, funniest, wisest private-eye in the field."*

☐	A CATSKILL EAGLE	11132-3	$4.99
☐	CEREMONY	10993-0	$4.99
☐	CRIMSON JOY	20343-0	$4.99
☐	EARLY AUTUMN	12214-7	$5.99
☐	GOD SAVE THE CHILD	12899-4	$4.99
☐	THE GODWULF MANUSCRIPT	12961-3	$4.99
☐	THE JUDAS GOAT	14196-6	$4.99
☐	LOOKING FOR RACHEL WALLACE	15316-6	$4.99
☐	LOVE AND GLORY	14629-1	$4.99
☐	MORTAL STAKES	15758-7	$4.99
☐	PROMISED LAND	17197-0	$4.99
☐	A SAVAGE PLACE	18095-3	$4.99
☐	TAMING A SEAHORSE	18841-5	$4.99
☐	VALEDICTION	19246-3	$4.99
☐	THE WIDENING GYRE	19535-7	$4.99
☐	WILDERNESS	19328-1	$4.99

*The Houston Post